The Modern Woman's Guide

To Online Dating

by

Lucy Garroway

The Modern Woman's Guide

To Online Dating

First Paperback Edition: September 2022

First Digital Edition: September 2022

Preface

Firstly, let me say that I am no expert in online dating although I have done more than my fair share. In my experience, the people who found happiness in relationships that started online were those girls who loved their lives and had stopped trying to look so hard for someone. If you think you're great then you are probably ready. If not then work on loving yourself because hey, no matter who you are... you are amazing.

Life has a way of putting people and things in our lives at the right time. We just might not realise it at that time.

Contents

Chapter One

Coastguard Cottages

H annah snapped out of her daydream and turned off the sad tune playing on the radio.

"Sunday Love Songs!" she objected. "More like heart wrenching torture songs!"

Suddenly she gasped, as she caught sight of the large ductile face pressed to the passenger window which slowly disappeared behind an increasing circle of mist made by two vacuous nostrils.

"Oh it's Francis!" she reassured herself, as she returned a smile and a chuckle to the comical face. She fumbled her way out of the car grabbing her phone, bag and a paper cup with the remnants of cold coconut milk cappuccino from the 24hour coffee bar, where she had just spent an hour alone.

Diane lived next door. Hannah called her Francis as she mistakenly thought that was her name and Diane had never corrected her.

"Good morning Francis. How are you?"

"You can park over at the wall you know. The couple who used to live there parked over at the wall." said Diane. She flicked her head sending her thick black floppy fringe to one side so she could peer out from behind it. Her green eyes were intensified by the swaying green dress that she wore, and her grey roots created an interesting contrast with the jet-black dye in her hair and eyebrows. Hannah thought to herself how odd that her upper lip hair appeared to remain naturally thick and black or perhaps she dyed that too. She was an oddity, but her overwhelmingly warm smile left you under a spell, that you could not resist and just had to smile back. She could tell you that she had killed your cat and you would forgive her if she smiled while doing it!

Diane had routines and a strong opinion on how she believed things should be done. Regular letters would appear through Hannah's letterbox, saying such things as 'for access purposes three metres should be left free beside the car (belonging to number 10) and the courtyard wall for access of emergency vehicles. Any visitors should be made aware of this and adhere to this

2

rule.' She would always end the letter stating that any further discussion on this matter should be referred to her solicitor, to whom she was passing on a copy of the letter. Then she would sign Ms D Sullivan. Diane would never speak in person of any of the issues she raised in letter form, and if Hannah dared mention any, she would allow the floppy fringe to drop over her eyes and shuffle away mumbling "Oh no, I don't know anything about that".

Diane lived alone as did most of the neighbours in the building. It was an old structure built in the 1800s as a coastguard station. The coastguard in those days were more like police, collecting taxes from the merchant ships that entered the harbour. It was now Coastguard Cottages. It had been divided into terraced houses with two apartments at one end. Diane and Hannah had an entrance to the front and rear of their houses, but the others had only one entrance at the back of the building. They all shared a path that passed through each garden, so a sense of community, that was like that of distant times, existed between the residents. The building was steeped in history and now was the dwelling place of an eccentric group of individuals.

Diane lived on one side of Hannah and Dave lived on the other. Dave was a very large, round man who liked to wear a suit and a green frayed woolly hat. He was partially deaf and lived alone. He kept a bicycle in his garden that he never rode.

Next to Dave was George. George was retired. He didn't drive or even seem to walk anywhere. George was married. His wife would leave the house sometimes, but George never went with her. George liked birds. He spent almost every day in the garden, watching the bull finches on his birdfeeders and pruning his plants. As soon as anyone entered their garden George was there talking about birds and the state of the drainage system since they raised the road in 1968.

Next to George lived the newcomers Sharon and George. George and George were rivals. Perhaps because they shared the same name. Afterall nobody wants to be George number two.

In the bottom apartment lived Grace. Grace had stage three cancer. She would sit just outside her front door, drinking herbal tea in her Greta Garbo wig. Always in the shade away from the sun's rays to protect her skin, which had been made sensitive by chemotherapy.

4

Above Grace lived Anthony. Nobody really knew Anthony very well apart from saying the obligatory "Hello" and comment on the weather. He had his career and two very nice cars, and it seemed as though that was all he needed.

Hannah and Diane had a strange relationship. Anyone else might dislike Diane with the frequent letters and demands but Hannah saw a bit of herself in Diane. Or at least she saw her future if she remained alone.

"Thank you for the rose-cuttings Francis. They have taken and are starting to grow," said Hannah as she searched her bunch of keys for the correct one to unlock her front door. 'I really must get rid of those old keys' she thought to herself, as she flipped the keys from her last three rented homes, round the keyring to the correct key. It was Hannah's first proper home. She had saved for years to buy a house that she belonged in but had nothing left to fix it up with. She was so proud when she looked at the tall chimney pots and large sash windows. "Like a grand old house, only in miniature" she would say. She waved goodbye to Diane who by now was singing in another world altogether. She used her broom as a dance partner as she brushed up leaves, some

5

rolling under her dress as it swished around the paved ground. As Hannah turned the key and stepped inside, she couldn't help wondering if the house was a home simply for one, and she would always live there alone, just like Diane.

Chapter Two

The Profile

Hannah had no intention of being a lonely old cat or chihuahua woman. She decided to change her mood and give her attitude a positive kick up the backside. She poured a generous glass of wine, although it was early and while she wouldn't normally drink before dinner time, she needed some Dutch courage. She flipped a switch, dropped the needle on to her favourite Louis Armstong LP and quickly lit the logs that were already in place in the fire and two cherry scented candles. Then, curled up on the sofa with her phone in her hand and took a large swig of wine before opening a new dating app. She hadn't dated anyone in such a long time, so she was feeling wildly apprehensive and awkward. She took another large gulp of wine. Unfortunately, she became intoxicated quite quickly when drinking wine, so she was being prudent and pacing herself.

"Butler!" she called out and a little black dog with white paws and a white patch like a cravat on his chest came bounding in through the door, skidded on the varnished wooden floor and leapt up onto the sofa, snuggling down beside her. "Ok Butler ... if I'm going to do this, I'm going to need your advice", she said, looking at Butler for moral support and wafting away his gammy breath with her hand.

Hannah began to create a profile using a selfie she had taken while on a short road trip around the coast. 'Outdoor lighting is always best for selfies', she thought. She had taken two selfies that day and while she could have used the one with the waves crashing over the rocks in the background, she opted for the one in which she was being terrorised by sheep. The sheep had surrounded her as they seemed to be warning her off their grazing area by stamping their hooves, gathering closely round her and bleating aggressively. Hannah felt the smile with a little terror had much more 'sexy chick' potential. "Nobody would know just by looking at my face that they had turned their backs to poop and toss it towards me with their rapidly swinging tails" she laughed to herself as she took a sip of wine. She decided it was a good decision. She wanted to look more serious in the rugged landscape, rather than smiling lethargically to the sound of the sea and squinting with the sun in her eyes.

She showed the photo to Butler. "What do you think Butler? Is this one ok?" Butler growled revealing his cute tiny little fangs. He didn't like any creatures bigger than himself excluding all children and female adult humans. People would stop and say "Aww, our dog has found a little friend", and after Butler finished sniffing the other dogs dangling bits and bum hole, he would go for their throats like a possessed vampire dog.

"It's ok little man" she reassured him patting his little head "they didn't hurt me." She reached for the bottle and poured herself another glass of wine then answered the usual questions about height, location, hair colour, hobbies etc.

"Now what shall we put in this section? Let's see…describe yourself and what you are looking for. This might take some time." Hannah closed her eyes for a moment and reflected on her best attributes and things she would like to do. It wasn't the first time she had set up a dating profile.

I love long drives with good music and a comfy coffee shop at the end of it. My sense of humour is possibly a little bit sarcastic. I completely acknowledge that I am not always right. I do quite a bit of DIY and am quite independent. I always win at board games.

I love to travel on a budget and experience different cultures. I care about the environment, equality and good manners. I would like to find someone like minded. I enjoy Sci-fi movies.

I am in no hurry and am more than happy to begin with a friendship.

"Well, that didn't take too long after all! Anyway, it's sort of honest… but maybe too serious? I wonder if I should put a joke in?" Not many people got Hannah's sense of humour, but she didn't get most other people's sense of humour either. That didn't put her off trying. Slowly butchering a joke, painfully ripping the guts out of it and squashing them right back up its nostrils and resulting in an awkward silence. Unfortunately, awkward silences sometimes made her laugh uncontrollably, not a good look following a joke homicide.

With her profile completed it was time to swipe right or left on the pics of some of the guys. She hesitantly tapped on the "meet" icon.

A photo appeared on her screen. It was of a man of about fifty years old, who was in a dark room, with his face lit up by his phone's flash, which was reflected in his large thick glasses. He was not smiling. Revealed below the pic was his profile name, unrealistic age of 38 years, and location. Hannah looked at Butler, "I don't think Ringo is my type!" she said followed by a sigh and a hiccup. As she swiped left, she began to wonder if dating apps were the best place to find her future companion in life.

Frank looked too much like a serial killer. Philip looked lost. John was too short. Joseph was 19 and looked cold with his shirt off! She needed another drink.

"At last," she sighed "someone who looks quasi-normal". She swiped right for Stuart. Left for the guy lying on his unhygienic looking sofa, and the guy who thought a pic of an expensive red car was better than his face. Then, three more right swipes. She was on a roll. By now she had some impressive thumb action going on and was making superficial judgements on dozens of guys in the blink of an eye.

Eventually, a notification dropped down from the top of her screen with a ping. Scott had sent her a message. "Oh!" she gasped "Let's see!" Her eyes lit up as she tapped on the 'messages' icon swaying slightly to one side with a tipsy flush of heat.

I must say, you have taken my breath away!
You are beautiful!

That was the message from Scott. She blushed and turned her phone away for a moment as though she believed he could see her, then she tapped on his tiny pic to open his profile and read all about him. He was an incredibly attractive guy in Kaki. Tall (6'2"), short dark hair, perfectly sized subtle tattoos on his large biceps and smiling in no less than three pics! He was from California and bless his cotton socks, a widower!

Hannah held her hands to her hot cheeks and shrieked! She couldn't believe the first guy to get in touch was a 'hottie'. She took to her feet and sang along to 'Mac the Knife' at the top of her voice, shaking her ass and dancing without rhythm around the room.

Abruptly, the needle reached the end of the record making a repetitive scratching noise. She flipped it, placed the needle very carefully to the beginning of side two with only one slight scratch, and flopped back down on the sofa. She composed herself, so that she could make a respectable and a sensibly sincere reply. "Well Mr Scott! Thank you for your kind words. I'm sure you deserve a bigging up too." She giggled to herself.

She held her thumbs in situ above the phone keypad, took a deep breath in and then exhaled. Then, she took another deep breath. And another. She stared at her phone a little dazed. Her eyes swivelled round to the snoring dog lying on his back with his legs in the air and his tongue hanging down one side of his face. "Thanks for nothing" she scorned. She knew she wanted her message to be polite, witty, charming, slightly flirty but most of all prompt. He had already waited for two thirds of Mac the Knife and could soon be messaging one of the other available girls online and in the running for Scott's affection. She was making herself anxious and in a moment of panic she typed...

Thank you (smiley face)

Before she could overthink it, she sent the disappointingly short message. "Any reply is better than nothing", she disbelievingly reassured herself. Her phone pinged again. This time the notification announced that she had messages from three different guys. She hesitated. Should she wait for Scott reply to her useless message? She decided to view the other messages to pass time while she waited for Scott to finish typing and send her message. She supped some more wine.

David was first. It was a simple "Hello". Hannah replied with an unimaginative but adequate 'Hello'.

Hello

Hello

Are you single?
My name is David

Isn't everyone single on here?
Are you single?

I am single

Me too (smiley face)

"What a palaver" she whispered to herself, just in case David might hear. "This is the very reason I detest small talk!"

Good.
Would you like to chat with me?

Hannah though it was best to check his profile first. His pic was taken at a beach. He was wearing shorts, a t-shirt, trainers and sunglasses. He was quite plain, 6' tall, lived in a town quite close by, never smoked, liked a drink occasionally, and spoke German and English. His profile personal description read 'Hello'. He had four more pics, one of which showed him holding a baby only a few weeks old.

I don't have long.
I'm about to make lunch.

Hannah winced feeling paranoid that David could see her somehow and disappointed in herself for the dishonesty as really, she was saving herself to chat with sexy Scott. She moved into the kitchen and turned the oven on to preheat satisfying

15

herself that now she really was about to make
lunch.

But sure.

How long have you been single?

Over 3 years now

How long have you been dating?

Too long

Were you married?

Never married but got engaged.
She broke my heart after six years.

"Hmm". Hannah decided that was all that she
needed to know about that. It had the potential to
turn into an epic retelling of a life story. She
spiced it up with...

So why do you think you haven't
met the right person yet?

Cheated on lots of women.
Been away for six months.
Two-year relationship fell apart.

You've cheated with lots of women?

Yes

No offence David but you don't

16

sound like the best characters if
you are cheating on people

Hard to trust anyone anymore

Ok. Well nice chatting
and good luck finding someone

Perhaps David was drunk. Matt was next. He was quite good looking with dark hair and a groomed beard. He was wearing a green shirt with two opened top buttons. His description section read 'Please don't be a fun sponge', Hannah didn't get it. He was 6'5". At the bottom were two more pics. A cute one with what must have been his daughter of around three years, and one with his face with a pint of beer in front of it. Hannah thought he looked safe enough for her to open his message.

Hey Hey (love emoji)
How're you doin'? x

Not impressed by his profile Hannah felt Matt deserved a reply of:

Hi Matt.

The full-stop being a sign that Hannah was not impressed and giving him the warning to up his game or leave now. He continued with his inadequate pursuit.

Hey Hannah, what are you up to? X

> *I'm on my phone...*
> *Messaging you*

Haha! As am I (sideways laughing emoji)

Hannah decided she had given Matt enough of her time.

Candidate number four was Brendan. Quite good-looking, wearing a hoodie and a slightly receding hairline. A consultant surgeon or at least that's what his profile read.

A notification alerted Hannah to a message from Scott.

"Sorry Brendan..." she said to the photo of the Doc "don't have time to read your message. I must reply to Scott forthwith." By now Hannah had her slightly drunken 'knight in shining armour' romantic head on.   Nobody would compare to the dashing Scott.

Want to get off this crazy site
 and chat properly?
Can I have your number?

Hannah hesitated for a moment.   What harm could possibly come from giving out her number?   If he should reveal himself as a serial killer, she could simply block him.   She typed her number and hit send.   She hadn't imagined when she was creating her profile that she would be giving her number so freely this soon.   Within seconds of sending her number his first text message came through.   Hannah ran to the kitchen, threw a frozen lasagne in the oven and quickly filled a glass of water.   She wanted to sober up and have sensible conversation with Scottie Boy!   And it was only lunchtime. "Hiccup!"

Hi Hannah
It's Scott.

Hi Scott

Why are you on that site and
how long have you been on there?

                              I just joined
                    It seems a little creepy

Tell me about the experience
you have had on there.

       Hannah felt there was not much to tell. She had basically created a profile, swiped a lot of pics left and right, replied to a few messages and here she was. She hoped the conversation was going to get more interesting. She covered herself by saying she had only just started to use the app and hadn't much experience. She was overcompensating with being sensible as she attempted to talk soberly and come across as not having much experience at online dating. And anyway, it could be difficult to think of things to say or questions to ask so she wanted to wait until Scott asked a question she could get into and get the conversation moving in an interesting direction.

Can I get to know more about you
if you do not mind?

Hannah was a little disappointed. The questions seemed very formal and if she was being honest a little boring. While Hannah was happy sharing information, she thought it would be best to ask a few questions of her own. Like...

Why don't you have a profile pic on Watsapp?

And all at once, the pic of Scott from the dating app appeared on his Watsapp profile. Hannah was relieved.

*Ahh hello ...
feel like I'm talking to
an actual person now.
So how long have you
been on the dating app?*

*I am new to that site
and you were my first match.
I was not feeling comfortable in there so that is
why I asked for us to chat here.
You can stop using that site now
and give me the chance to get to know
you better and let us see how it goes.*

Oh that's ok.

I have given up on it already.
I would like to know more about
your relationship status,
what you do for a living, hobbies,
what you do for fun, favourite food
and favourite colour.

Hannah paused. She didn't enjoy talking all about herself. She felt two-way conversation would be more productive than a questions and answer session. She was wary of telling too much about herself before she was comfortable that guys she talked to weren't married and trying to have an affair or that they were the age they stated and did actually look like their photos. She had heard so many stories recently about people not being who they were portraying online. She decided to give him the benefit of the doubt, but she would proceed with an unclear head caution. Scott was worth that. She answered and then turned the tables on him. He had to answer the same questions now. She used the time as he typed to topple her lasagne out on to a plate and tried to rush eating it. The hot red sauce was like lava on her tongue, so she put ice in her water to cool her scorched taste buds.

I'm a widower with no kids.
I lost my wife and only kid to an accident
in California 2 years ago.
She got drunk on her birthday and
drove herself and the kid into a pit
because I couldn't make it home from deployment.

      Hannah almost choked on the last piece of dry sauceless pasta as she read. Goosebumps tingled all over her body and she became uncomfortable at the seriousness of what Scott had just revealed to her. He didn't linger on it but went on to say that he was a first lieutenant in the US Marines and that he was simply looking for someone to spend his life with. She avoided asking anything that would distress him and reinstated the wine. He didn't seem to dwell on his tragic past but spoke about what he wanted for his future. He asked some more questions about her, so she told him about her house, which she loved, and when she had moved to the town she lived in, and what had drawn her to the place. He talked to her about California and his life there. It all sounded so different and more exciting than what Hannah was used to. They chatted with ease

23

the whole day and late into the night and Hannah decided to turn off notifications from the dating app, which had continued to pop up on her phone. Surprisingly Scott seemed to get her sense of humour and she relished in his compliments and gentle flirting. She dropped off to sleep mid-text and snored through the most glorious night's sleep.

Chapter Three
Online Chat

The next morning Hannah took Butler on his early morning walk and fed him his breakfast as usual. He was drinking his water to wash down his healthy but bland kibble and almost choked when he suddenly began to bark and growl in the direction of the front door. The loud clangour of the brass sprung letterbox reverberated around Hannah's throbbing head and alerted her to check for mail.

"Shh Butler... it's ok. Just the letterbox." She reassured him as he continued his territorial high-pitched rant. She opened the door to the porch and stepped onto the cold stone tiles with her bare feet and looked down to find a small pink envelope on the royal blue welcome mat. "Francis..." she sighed. It was addressed to Number 10. It was a polite complaint about the loud singing during Hannah's euphoric demonstration at receiving a message from Scott the day before. She blushed at the cheesiness of her behaviour then cringed with the punishing pain in her head from last night's wine. She decided to apologise to Francis next time she bumped into her. It would, however, be difficult as Francis would never acknowledge sending her own letters or any of the issues that she had raised in them with Hannah. "One would imagine that she hadn't been the one to send the letters! Perhaps it isn't Francis at all?" Hannah spoke aloud, as she considered that maybe it was another personality that shares Francis' body, like in an old movie that she had seen. While one personality is conscious the other sleeps. It's a real condition and Hannah is open to all possibilities, as she herself had an imaginary friend as a child, or at least that's what her mother had told her.

"I wonder how she always gets to the front door and can post the letters in and get away without me ever seeing her? Also, I wonder why she always signs her letters with the initial 'D' instead of 'F'. There's certainly something mysterious about her," said Hannah, still talking to herself, as she would often do, then instantly remembered the old fashioned saying that it was the first sign of madness. She disagreed with this

26

sentiment and thought if more people spoke out loud exactly what they were thinking, the world would be a more peaceful place with less pent-up anger.

Hannah's living room window overlooked her front door which was at a right angle to it. She had been caught in awkward positions by many delivery guys because of this. It seemed impossible for Diane to post a letter without being seen.

After her breakfast Hannah checked her phone and as expected there was a reply to the message that she had sent Scott when she awoke that morning. She had apologised for falling asleep during their conversation. She explained that she was just on her way out to work and would look forward to chatting with him later. He, of course, was apologetic for keeping her up so late and demonstrated good manners and charm at every opportunity.

Later, Hannah discretely checked her phone again, on her break during work. There were no messages from Scott, but she had been the one to say she would be chatting to him later, so couldn't really blame him for anything, even though she was a little disappointed. She decided that there was no point trying to begin a conversation with him on her break with such little time, so instead she opened the dating app to see what she had been missing.

She had so many messages from so many guys. This was all very unexpected, however she had experienced something similar a few years ago when she tried online dating. It seems everyone wants to pounce on the new guy and are only interested until the next new guy comes along. Hannah felt she should at least read the messages, as they had gone to the trouble of writing to her, and she had nothing better to do while she munched on her strawberry yogurt with homemade cinnamon granola. She slurped her Earl Gray tea and tapped on the earliest message.

Olivier was French but lived within 50 miles of Hannah in a village that she had never heard of.

Hi, nice to meet you.
I didn't find your Facebook wall. Why?
Because I am fed up about fake (sad emoji)

She thought she had better reply. After all he seemed bewildered by his experience on the dating app, or perhaps he was just grumpy. By any measure he was obviously disgruntled by his negative experience, and she felt bad for him. Olivier was not online, so she left a quick message asking what a Facebook wall was and where Frankborough was and moved on to the next eligible bachelor.

Rob's profile pic was very interesting. He was sitting beside a large blue plastic box with a lid on it. Out from one side poked a little grey head with jet black eyes and stubby whiskers. He was a seal rescue worker! The seal was cute. The guy was … ok. He had a blonde beard with a Gunslinger moustache. His head was shaven, and he had bright blue eyes. One of his other pics showed him with a magpie chick in his hand and a Walrus moustache. Another showed him lying head-to-head with a cocker spaniel and a Horseshoe moustache. "He's obviously an animal lover" Hannah concluded, as she munched on a handful of salted cashew nuts. There was little info on his profile, and he had made no attempt to fill in the description.

Hey Hannah.
How's things?

Any plans for the weekend?

Hannah left a reply for him to read next time he was online.

> *Sorry I didn't get back to you sooner Rob.*
> *I work weekends.*
> *Mondays and Tuesdays are my days off.*
> *Your work looks very interesting!*

Enough said. Hannah moved on to the next message in her inbox. Wayne was an active guy. His profile pic showed him finishing a marathon. Another pic showed him in a wetsuit (waist up). Another was at the top of a mountain, and another was receiving an award wearing a suit and tie. He was 5'11". Didn't smoke. Drank occasionally and lived about 30 miles away. He had no description. He was of athletic build, plenty of black hair, clean shaven and a nice smile.

Heya Hannah how r u? X

> *Hi Wayne, I'm good.*
> *How are you?*

Hannah checked the time. She just had enough time for one more reply. Bruno was Portuguese, 5'9", an engineer, never smoked, drank occasionally and spoke Portuguese, English and Spanish. His hobbies included cooking, DIY projects, Model Cars, travelling, Yoga and watching movies.

Hi, Hannah, how are you keeping? (Smiling emoji)
Happy Friday! (Smiling emoji)
and if not too late Happy new year! (5ᵗʰ April)

Hi Bruno,
Sorry I missed your message.
Yes, it is too late for Happy New Year.
Would love to chat another time.
(Smiley face)

Hannah glanced over her shoulder to check there wasn't anybody sitting too closely behind her, closed the app and popped her phone in her pocket. She had a subtle spring in her step as she returned to her work, quite pleased with her level of popularity. This boost was just what she needed. She found replying to all sorts of guys from different backgrounds great fun.

That evening Hannah elected for an early night. She grabbed a take-away on her way home and this evenings after dinner entertainment was going to be chatting to Scott. A virtual date! She changed into her silky pjs, fluffy socks, cosy dressing gown and made herself comfortable surrounded by her plumped up pillows.

Hey Scott
How's things?

Hannah, I have been excited
to hear from you all day.
Tell me all about your day.
Was it good?

Hannah was so excited by his prompt reply. She told Scott briefly about her day, but she wanted to talk about something much more important. She wanted to meet Scott, so suggested it again. However, it was not to be as straight forward an answer as she had hoped.

I have explained Hannah that
I am enlisted here for 6-8 weeks
depending on how long the project takes.

After that I am all yours and we can
see each other as often as we like.

> *I don't usually tell someone so much*
> *about myself before we meet, as a rule.*
> *If we meet and there is no spark, we*
> *have learned a lot about each other for nothing.*
> *Imagine if it happened with everyone*
> *that you sent a message to*

I have explained this to you Hannah.
I want to get to know you while I am
unable to meet you, and this is the only way.
Do you not trust me?
Why do you think I would invest all
this time talking to only you?

Hannah didn't know how to take Scott's words. She read over his messages in two very different tones. Firstly, in a soft reassuring and perhaps slightly patronising tone. Then, with a little aggression. Was this just their first argument or was something more sinister going on? She reflected back to what he had told her about his wife. Maybe she had killed herself because he was controlling, or she was depressed and told him she

33

needed him, and he had rejected her cries for help. What could drive a woman to such a thing? Was Hannah just overreacting? She decided she was being unduly dramatic. It was the result of her being frustrated, because six to eight weeks seemed so far away it might as well be six to eight years! Unfortunately, her impetuous side took over.

I'm sorry Scott.
I feel that things might be
getting too complicated.
Texts can be read in different ways,
and it is difficult to know
how to read them sometimes.
If we build a picture of each
other over such a long time
and it is not true to life,
there will only be disappointment.

Hannah, I have explained to you
why I cannot meet for now.
This is the only way we must
get to really know each other.

I'm sorry Scott but I

don't think we would be suited.
I hope you find someone
to make you happy.

I'm sorry you feel that way Hannah.
I thought we could be something real and special.
I am just looking for someone to love and care for
And to be loved in return.
I wish you every happiness in your search for love.

Hannah read Scott's last message and then instantly panicked that she had been too hasty. Her heart plunged down low in her chest, painfully beating with uncertainty and disappointment. But it was too late. She had to let Scott go. What if she was making one of the biggest mistakes of her life? What if he was the perfect man for her and she never met anyone that she could ever live happily with and she missed the opportunity to find him. These encounters don't happen every day. They had bonded so quickly over texting, and she felt like she knew him, and she had told him all about herself and was able to say anything she thought or felt. She had acted without thinking it through properly. A silly lovers tiff! Could she quickly message him and say she was happy to wait, or would that just be embarrassing and needy? She wrestled in the moment with having been too harsh and stubborn

It was emotionally hard work trying to make sensible decisions. She must put things in perspective and stop acting dramatically. If it was meant to be with Scott then things would have worked out and it would have been fate, and out of her control. Unfortunately, she didn't believe in fate. At least not anymore. She went through a phase of thinking everything was determined and left things up to fate a few years ago and it got her nowhere, ergo she changed her mind on that theory. So? She was fickle... only a slight flaw!

She was not going to be deterred. It was a setback but that was the world of online dating. She might have felt dejected and disappointed at how her virtual date night had gone but there was a long list of messages in her inbox and what better way to take her mind off Scott's charismatic smile and brawny biceps. She took a deep breath and curiously opened her inbox in hope of cheering herself up with some amusement and maybe even some new possibilities.

Chapter Four
First Date

Hannah whipped up the brown silky froth of her hot chocolate with the tip of her little finger and sucked it off it with a popping sound. She snuggled down again into her bed, put her headphones on, selected the 'Romantic Moods' playlist she had compiled two years ago on a good day and readied herself to find a man worthy of a date. No more wasting time with too much chat and fancy ideas of hot GI Joes with charming smiles and a tragic dark side. The time had come for sensible and genuine. So what if someone is a little short, or bald, or had one eye looking at you while the other was looking for you.

The voluminous list of messages, placed in front of her, was slightly overwhelming for Hannah. She couldn't possibly reply to everyone but what if the perfect guy was hidden in there somewhere? She looked for an interesting face or kind expression.

She was drawn to the French guy. She was in a romantic mood and although she denied it to herself, she was allowing herself to be influenced by stereotypes. She recalled asking him where Frankborough was located. His reply was a county a good distance from Hannah.

You are quite far away.

Nooooo,

it is you who are quite far LOL

She was disappointed that the distance meant a relationship would be impractical, however, it narrowed down the number of contenders, so she moved on.

Rob the seal rescuer had replied.

Hi Hannah
Sorry to disappoint you but
I am a plain old engineer for work.
The seal rescue I do as a volunteer.
Although I am better qualified than
most that get paid for it.

Rob was online so Hannah chatted to him happily for about ten minutes and they found they had lots in common. However, it was time to talk to other guys now too. Hannah admittedly did not have impeccable multi-tasking talents, but she felt confident enough to be able to start another conversation and jump back and forth to the conversation with Rob without him noticing.

There had been a few messages from Bruno sent at different times despite the fact she had not replied to most of them. She admired his persistence. To her surprise, in the last message from him he suggested going for a walk sometime. Hannah grinned smugly and inhaled the chocolatey vapours before taking a large satisfying slurp of hot chocolate. She wiped the steam from her skinny black rimmed reading glasses and got straight to typing a reply.

*Maybe we could go
for a coffee instead?*

*Your photos are beautiful
Hannah!
I defo vote for a walk!*

Hannah decided she was becoming fatigued with chatting online. Scott had taught her a lesson. There was no point talking to anyone she found attractive if there was a chance they would never meet. She chatted briefly with Rob about sea-life and then made her apologies saying she must walk Butler. Then she got back to Bruno.

A walk would be lovely Bruno
but it's dark and cold outside.
A coffee would be much better.

Tonight?
Let's go for coffee tonight?
LOL (smiley face)

Ok. Where?

Hannah had surprised, not only Bruno, but herself by her spontaneity. They arranged to be at a coffee shop halfway between their two homes within 45 minutes.

Sure (smiley face)
See you soon (double smiley faces)

Hannah leapt from her bed. She had ten minutes to put on clothes, apply some makeup and start the car.

Twelve minutes later Hannah was sitting in the driver's seat. She wished for Bruno to be less efficient with time and arrive after her at the coffee shop. On this occasion Hannah made it to her destination with minutes to spare. The lights were all green, the roads surprisingly clear, but Hannah's driving was made more proficient by her competitive streak. Unfortunately, mild road rage was one of her few flaws. She performed better at everything that presented a challenge to her and she wanted to get there before Bruno so he would have to be the one to find her. She didn't want to have to identify him in a crowd.

She hurried inside and went straight to the counter, ordering her usual cappuccino with coconut milk and a dusting of chocolate powder, then had a quick glace around. There were no guys sitting on their own and because the building was mainly glass, she could see that nobody was approaching either.

Hannah's coffee was ready within a few minutes. She made her way to the table in the corner which was surrounded by empty tables.

She removed her coat and sat down. Taking out her phone she had another quick look outside but still nobody was approaching the coffee shop. Now he was a few minutes late. That gave her enough time to quickly check his profile and their past conversation. Now she felt ready. Two girls came into the coffee shop whispering and giggling. They stood by the counter. Hannah hoped they wouldn't choose to sit at one of the tables next to hers.

At last, a guy walked in. This must be him. He waved. Relief. It was him. Bruno. Hannah had begun to worry that he wasn't going to show up at all. She waved back. He had a warm smile. Fortunately, while he stood waiting for the giggling girls to decide which slice of cake they would share, Hannah had time to size him up. He was a little taller than Hannah. He wore a kaki trench coat with a stripey scarf so she couldn't see his figure exactly but from what she could see he was a nice build.

He had light brown skin, thick dark eyebrows, and a little stubble. He too looked over at her with sneaky glances when he thought she wasn't looking. With each glance he would try to take in something more of Hannah's appearance. By now the giggling girls were getting on Hannah's nerves. They were holding up her date. Fortunately for Hannah, she had a seat and could comfortably watch Bruno, until a slow reaction on her part meant they caught each other's eyes. Bruno smiled and made gestures for her amusement. He attempted his own form of sign language. He pulled faces at the girls behind their backs. He danced a robotic performance of making his own coffee. Each time one of the girls turned his way he would freeze mid-move. Hannah laughed. A little bond formed between them as they communicated across the coffee shop with languages that didn't involve words. The girls lifted their tray carrying their coffees and treat and turned to Bruno giving him a mean girl look. Bruno looked at Hannah and gave her a wink, sealing their united condescension of giggly youth and its distain at the ability of anyone, other than members of their pack, to have fun.

In the course of time, Bruno had his coffee and was walking quite confidently towards the table. "Hi, I am Bruno. I am sorry I am late. I was sure I would arrive first as you left so little time to get ready." Bruno said playfully in a soft cheery Portuguese accent. He removed his coat and scarf to reveal a tight dark blue t-shirt and jeans. He had a toned body and was happy to display it. "I'm Bruno." He announced again as he sat down.

"I'm sorry you had to wait so long for your coffee. I should have checked what you like, and I could have ordered it for you when I arrived." Hannah replied.

"I was surprised you wanted to meet up this evening! It was a nice surprise. And you choose to sit in the corner far from the nosey people that would want to know who we are and what we are doing meeting this time of night." He laughed. "Or you are being clever. You are cold and so you sit in the corner. You should always sit in the corner of a room when cold as a corner is always 90 degrees" Bruno jested.

Hannah didn't know anything about Bruno. She couldn't remember what she had read before he arrived, so she started straight into a question-and-answer session. He had moved here a few years back from Portugal with no money, no friends and few possessions. He had been given a job with a gaming publisher. The company had paid for one week of accommodation in a small hotel. Then he had moved into a room in a shared apartment with three girls. Two of which were a couple and had invited him to become a threesome.

"Too much information!" Hannah protested with a smile.

"I have lots of information and facts Hannah. I collect them so I may share them with you." Bruno leaned in across the table. "Do you know the sky at night is actually a muddy brown colour, but human eye is unable to see this colour, so we see black?"

"Oh, I will never look at the night sky the same again!" Hannah retorted. She liked interesting facts.

"Did you know otters hold hands while going down the river together, so they don't lose each other? They hold hands while they sleep too so they do not drift apart. True fact!" Bruno looked pleased with himself as Hannah looked very impressed with his knowledge, and the romantic theme of his fact. "Also, did you know your nipples are older than your teeth? Actually. It's a fact."

And with that, Hannah asked Bruno about his hobbies. As requested, he told Hannah about his love to build racing cars. Not life size cars but miniature ones. He fumbled around, for his phone, in his coat pocket. He showed Hannah photos of a newly produced chassis and the finished article which he had designed, assembled and spray painted. Bruno took it all very seriously. Hannah watched his face light up when he talked about the different cars that he had invested a lot of money in. "I joined a Facebook group, and we hold events all over the country for races about once a month."

"Do you wear headsets and shout out navigations to co-drivers like numbers and co-ordinates and stuff?" Hannah quipped.

"Hannah! You are laughing at me!"

Hannah grinned. "We do wear headsets actually. It can be a dangerous sport actually. There are many interesting things about my hobby actually." Hannah felt bad for having mocked him as he sat back looking like an injured child. "I am boring you."

"Oh no!" replied Hannah with an apologetic smile. "I think it is marvellous when people have interesting hobbies. I think it must be lovely meeting people who share an interest and competing makes it even more fun."

"You can come and stand track side and cheer me on. The others have wives and children who attend but I have no one."

"I'd like that." Hannah liked Bruno. He seemed funny and charming. She could just imagine herself track side applauding him while he made car engine revving and screeching brakes noises. She tried not to laugh at her thoughts as she didn't want to offend him further.

"I think you would enjoy it. I tell my Mama June about it and she always says she wishes that she could come see her little Bruno win the race!"

"Your Mama June?" Hannah asked.

"Yes. When I lived in the apartment with the girls. You remember I told you... they wanted a threesome..."

"Yes I remember," interrupted Hannah.

Bruno laughed. "What? You think maybe they would not find me irresistible? Or are you embarrassed? I did not do any sex with them."

"Yes, thank you Bruno" she interrupted again quite flabbergasted.

"You don't have to be jealous Hannah. I don't see them anymore and it was a few year ago now" he laughed seeing Hannah blush at his candour.

"Anyway, you were saying about your "Mama June"?"

"Oh yes! She lived in the next apartment. She liked me actually. I helped her to take out trash and carry heavy bag. She made me dinner sometimes and talked to me because I was so far from home and family. Her husband Jim, he always make her angry. He would joke. She would say he is lazy and useless, but I know they love each other very much. You know?" Hannah enjoyed listening to Bruno talk and could tell he was comfortable in her company. "They don't have any children of their own. I still visit or make a phone call to Mama June often. She is getting older now and I worry I am not close to help her."

"That must be very comforting to you... to have someone who enjoys hearing your news?" Hannah smiled.

"Yes, I visited them last week and was telling them I had a date with a French girl. Jim asked how she was in bed! Just like that. Mama June threw a pot and it hit him on the head! Actually!" Bruno laughed as he reminisced, but Hannah was a little vexed by the mention of sex again and more over another girl and only last

48

week. She promptly moved the conversation on. "So what do you do when you aren't racing, working or going on dates?". Hannah's tone revealed a little jealousy. Bruno had a cheeky grin and a glint in his eyes. "Actually, I tell interesting facts and give good advice. Like do you know that towels are the biggest cause of dry skin? And did you know that many many years ago when poor people saved their urine in a pot to sell for tanning leather some could not afford a pot. So actually, they were so poor they did not have a pot to piss in. That is where the saying comes from. I do not have a pot to piss in. Ha! True fact!" Hannah shook her head as if to scold him as she tried not to laugh at his beguiling misbehaviour. "Just one more." He pleaded. "A man who walks through an airport turnstile sideways is going to Bangkok. Very true." Bruno let out a hearty laugh and Hannah couldn't resist laughing along with his alluring boyish display. He cleared his throat and with a forced serious face began a serious conversation about his favourite movies and box sets he had enjoyed watching. He recommended some for Hannah that he thought she might like, as he recalled reading that she liked sci-fi in her profile.

The waiter brushed the floor around their table. Hannah looked around to discover the coffee shop was empty. They had been caught up in chatting and hadn't noticed it was almost closing time. The barista turned off the music which had been playing quietly in the background. "I think they want us to leave" Hannah whispered. Bruno stood up immediately and flung his coat around his shoulders.

"Oh, we're leaving!" Hannah too stood up, donned her coat and made her way towards the door, which Bruno was holding open waiting for her to exit. They moved outside into the cold windy night. Hannah's hair lifted up twirling in the blustery air, so she placed her hands either side of her head to hold it back from her face. "Well, that's my car over there. Where's your car?" she asked. Hannah didn't enjoy partings of any kind. A brief goodbye and a concluding "thanks I had a lovely time", as she walked away was her usual routine._ As a rule, it was always best to avoid any physical interaction or the inappropriate 'do you want to see me again' question, until she had reviewed the date in her own time.

"My car is over there." He said, as he suddenly stretched his arms out wide and moved towards a befuddled Hannah. She tried to take a step backwards but Bruno with his coat bellowing in the wind like batman's cape swiftly enveloped a recoiling Hannah. She tried to utter words in a plea to escape but could only stutter "I... I..." Time seemed to move to slow motion and her eyes bulged as she saw Bruno's fat lips squashed up into a juicy pucker moving in towards hers. There was nothing she could do to avoid the impending kiss. She closed her eyes and flinched turning her head away, preventing the wet blubbery clams making contact with her lips, but instead landing in the webs of straggly hair covering her ear. He pulled his head back and strands of hair slid from between his lips coating them in saliva and whipping Hannah in the face on their release. She held her breath and wriggled free in a discombobulated mess. She recovered just enough to straighten up and say "thanks, I had a lovely time" as she turned and quickly marched with her head in quite a daze in the direction of her car. She didn't look back and the only thought repeating in the brain behind her red face was "I wish I had washed my hair". However, she had had enough embarrassing dates in the past that this one would still go down as one of the more successful ones.

She sat in her car and improvised looking for something in her glovebox, and checking her phone, as she sensibly waited for Bruno to drive off, just in case he followed her home and on the off chance he was a serial killer. "Phew!" she exhaled as she watched him drive out of sight. She debated with herself how the date went on the drive home. It fluctuated between very good and ok. By the time she arrived the verdict was a definite 'better than expected'. She decided she would really like to see Bruno again.

She took Butler for his night-time poop walk. The wind had settled down, the moon was almost full and high in the clear sky. As they strolled down the streetlamp lit path lined with trees, she told him all about her date. "I think you would like him Butler, he is funny and knows lots of interesting facts" she told him while trying to see the little dark creature who was camouflaged in the dappled shadows of broad branches. "He tried to kiss me you know!" she cried "but we won't talk about that. An encounter probably best forgotten. I don't think I will tell anyone about Bruno. I think it would be bad luck as I hope things might go well." Butler sneezed. "I knew you'd agree" Hannah said smiling and they turned to walk back home.

By the time Hannah was settled in her bed she realised she hadn't let Bruno know that she wanted to see him again and it was getting very late. She grabbed her phone but then hesitated. There was no message from him. Maybe he didn't want to see her again. She didn't want to seem overly eager either, especially if it was one sided. She had an idea. She texted him asking what the name of the show was that he had suggested for her to watch. He replied. She was relieved.

> *I'll watch the first episode*
> *as I fall asleep and*
> *I'll let you know*
> *what I think tomorrow.*

I look forward to it.
Good night Hannah x

> *Good night Bruno*

Chapter Five
Cold Tea

Hannah was up early as usual next morning. She had washed her hair, eaten breakfast and walked Butler through the memorial park. It was still dark and there was a frost sparkling on the ground. She was about to leave for work when her phone pinged. "Oh! Could this be Bruno?" she said excitedly as she took her phone out of her pocket. It was Scott.

Hannah
You might not want to hear from me right now, but I am texting in case you are feeling the same as me and don't want to leave things without at least finding out if we could have something real. I feel like we have a connection and understand each other, and it wouldn't be fair not to at least try.

I have so much love in me to give.
It can be hard to find real love in this
world and I don't want to miss what
could be the one opportunity.

Hannah was thrown. This was so
unexpected. He could be right. Perhaps he was
the one. How can we know if we have made the
right choices or missed important opportunities
in life? Maybe fate had sent Scott on his mission
to enable the two to meet. When she looked at
the images of him on her phone her heart
fluttered. She was sure if she had ever felt that
way before when she hadn't even met that
someone. Surely not a common occurrence for
people. But Hannah would have to wait weeks
to see him, and she was not a patient person. In
fact, impatience was one of her very few flaws.
There was too much to think about and she
would be late for work if she didn't leave soon.
Without giving him an answer, but biding herself
more time to think, she replied that she was
running late for work and would chat with him
later.

She thought about it all day and talked it
over with the girls in work. They agreed that he

was very attractive and thought what had happened to his wife was very distressing but didn't have much advice for her. It was up to Hannah to decide. What did she have to lose? She could continue to chat with other guys in the meantime to stop herself from getting carried away focusing on Scott while she made her mind up.

That afternoon after work, it was such a lovely sunny day that Hannah sat in the garden, despite having to wear a coat and scarf. The blackbirds were busy throwing old rotting leaves around and finding plenty of juicy bugs that were too tired or cold to run away in the wintery chill. Every now and then Butler would make a dash for them, just to remind them whose garden it was. There were very tall cherry blossoms and birch trees bordering her small plot, but it was too soon for leaves and the blossom were still only little buds, so the garden was drenched in sunshine. She drank earl grey tea from a floral cup and saucer to suit her mood.

"It's a lovely afternoon!!" she bellowed at the top of her voice. She was determined to catch Dave as he walked out of his door, for once he turned his back, he couldn't hear her if she blasted 'When the Saints come marching in' on a trumpet. "Yes lovely! Garden is looking well! Love the daffodils", he shouted, even though Hannah's hearing was perfectly fine. It was Dave that was tone deaf.

"Have a nice evening Dave!" she hollered while rolling her eyes, as he strolled off down the path oblivious. She was alerted to George number one being in his garden, with a raise of Dave's hand to wave, as he passed. She decided she should try not to think out loud while in the garden today. She sent her first message to Scott. Just a simple opener, as after this morning's message from him she needed an icebreaker.

Hey. How was your day?

> *It was ok but it is improving*
> *because you have texted me.*

What are you doing right now?

> *I am just sitting in the garden*
> *enjoying the sun and having*
> *a cup of tea. I have been thinking*
> *about what you said earlier, and I*

don't see why we couldn't continue
to chat and get to know each other a
little more.

This is very good news.
Would you do something
for me if I asked you to?

That depends on what it is?

Can you close your eyes and imagine
you are somewhere that makes you
happy? Imagine your perfect life.
What does that look like?

I don't need to close my eyes.
I am in my happy place.
It's my garden.

OK. So your garden is where you are now.
At your home where you live now.
But imagine something better.
A better more perfect life.
What would that be?

I'm sorry Scott I don't think you
understand. I am very content with my

life. I don't want anything better. Of course,
things could add to my life and I would welcome
them and I understand they could enrich my life
more but I am very happy. Someone to share my
life with would be wonderful but it is
not something I need. I like change
and I am very adaptable. I don't
need material things. So I'm not
really sure what you mean?

Please Hannah. Just do this thing for me.
Don't feel foolish. Just close your eyes.

Scott was quite persistent. Maybe Hannah
was being hard on him. Perhaps he was just a
romantic soul and wanted her to respond.
However, Hannah could not bring herself to do
it, even to humour him. She did not enjoy any
kind of meditation or overly serious mindfulness
and had bad experiences of it in the past. She
was asked to leave Pilates the first time she tried
it because she giggled when she was told to
stretch up and release her inner tree. To make
matters worse one of the participants had
flatulence. Once she started laughing, she just
couldn't stop and the more she tried to hide it

the worse it got. It wasn't that she was nervous or embarrassed. But rather that it was funny, and she didn't take life to seriously. Life was there to be enjoyed. Of course, there were bad times, sad times and things beyond her control, but she saw them as part of life and great learning experiences. She always considered herself very fortunate as some people past and present had horrendous lives full of hunger, pain, suffering and repression. She didn't need to force relaxation on herself. She had spent more than half her life daydreaming and that was sufficiently relaxing. She had to bite her lip to stop herself laughing at funerals, which is terribly taboo. Not because, as some great psychologists suggest, people get anxious and don't know how to handle their emotions which results in an inappropriate response, but because she listened to how the living talked about the deceased and how everyone looked so sad knowing fine well they will all be having a drink and a laugh as soon as the coffin is lowered. She would rather everyone would just lighten up and celebrate a person's life. She herself had no fear of death. No, she would not be convinced by Scott to do something that she did not want to do. She would feel she was being false. Making up some fake scenario that she believed he would be happy to hear, when the truth was, she was happy, and he could not convince her otherwise. If her life were any different, she couldn't know that she would be as happy as she was right now.

I'm sorry Scott. I really can't.
I don't wish to offend you but I
really don't have any wish for any
kind of better life so I don't see the point.
I was really just hoping for some
light-hearted conversation.

I just wanted you to do this one thing for me.
Why can't you understand I just want to
get to know you better?

But you are getting to know me better.
You know that I am happy and do not
want for anything more than what I
have. What is it that you want Scott?
What do you see when you close your eyes?

I feel that you are playing games
with me Hannah. I like you very

much and only want to get to know you.

Hannah felt the same uncomfortable feeling she had been made to feel by Scott before. Something just didn't feel right. She didn't want something so intense so soon. She had to do the unpleasant task of rejecting Scott again before her feelings developed even more. She was so disappointed. She was polite, apologetic and sincere. She blocked his number so she could not be tempted to correspond again. She sat with her cold tea and a sullen face. The shadows of the trees were cast long across the garden as the sun was low in the sky and the temperature was dropping further.

Suddenly she realised… "Bruno!" she had forgotten all about him. She called Butler and brought her cup and saucer inside to the warm kitchen. She began to prepare her dinner and texted Bruno in a badly done multitasking style with spelling mistakes and bad grammar. She had never been good at multitasking. She admitted that it was one of her very few flaws.

She apologised for having fallen asleep the night before about fifteen minutes into the show

he had recommended but tonight Bruno had a
new suggestion.

I want to watch the sad film
with you LOL. Then you get
sad and need a cuddle ;)
Good plan right?

Maybe

What do you mean maybe?
You will be fine with me.
Coffee with me last night
gave you new strengths. LOL

Oh it's not that I would be too
tired it's just that I don't know
you well enough to be in your
home alone with you. Sorry Bruno.
Maybe we can go for a walk like
you suggested before sometime before
it gets dark.

She was feeling a little down and didn't
much feel like talking to Bruno tonight. She left
her phone aside until she was getting into bed.
There were several messages from him. "I

suppose it shows he hasn't gone on a date with someone else so that's good" she reassured herself.

The idea of a strong man taking care of her a little had seemed appealing to her. Scott had stirred something in her she hadn't felt in a long time. She was alone. She looked after herself because there was nobody else around to support her. She had started to watch couples making decisions together, hugging each other, ordering drinks and food for each other because they know what the other likes. Why didn't she have that? She had nobody to share the bills with, to ask how her day went, to hold the ladder while she cleaned out the gutters or changed the light fittings. No-one to kiss goodnight. She thought maybe it was better to leave Bruno's messages until tomorrow. She was tired but restless. After tossing and turning unable to sleep for just under two hours she switched on her bedside lamp and fixed her pillows so she could sit up. Trying to force sleep was futile. She opened Bruno's messages to amuse herself. She giggled at his facts of when a woodpecker pecks wood it wraps its tongue around it's brain to prevent brain damage, and the longer you watch concrete the harder it gets. He saw she was online and immediately sent her a new message.

Missing me? (smiley face)

> *Yes Bruno (smiley face)*
> *It is lovely to read your messages*

You will miss me even more
when I fly to Dublin tomorrow
for a conference for a few days.

> *Well perhaps we can meet up for*
> *that walk when you get back.*

And with that they wished each other 'Good night' and Hannah dropped off in no time.

At 06.04am the next morning Hannah's phone pinged. Bruno had sent photos of himself looking tired and bored at the airport. It was early for him. He usually didn't get up until 8.30am as he worked from home most of the time.

Hannah drove into work early so she could have a coffee and relax before she started. She was disappointed not to have had more messages from Bruno, so she again had a look on the dating app. There were plenty of new messages, but she missed Scott a little, the little romantic talks they had and the feeling like they knew each other. She looked for his old messages simply to read over things they had talked about before she had given him her number. The messages weren't there. Not a trace as if they had never existed. She tried to find his profile in her Matches section. There was a notification on a blank profile stating a 'Match' had recently deleted their account. She knew that must have been Scott. What other reason could there be for the disappearance of his messages. Maybe he had deleted it when they had decided to chat outside of the app. She checked for his conversation in Watsapp. She had to open the archive section where she had moved to so she wouldn't be tempted to text him. His picture had disappeared. Perhaps there was another less innocent reason for all his secrecy. Perhaps Scott was married. Perhaps Scott wasn't his real name and Scott wasn't Scott at all! Perhaps she was being over dramatic and there was a perfectly simple explanation for it all.

She noticed the date and time of the last time he had been online was the time of her last message to him. Something just wasn't right! He had disappeared. She read over some of the conversation. He had spelt colour wrong. Americans spell it without the 'u'. She remembered being told this in computer class at school. The computer would auto correct to c-o-l-o-r because it was set up as American English instead of UK. She realised that when she read over his messages it just didn't seem how an American would phrase things or express themselves. The blood drained from her face. She felt an anxious nausea in the pit of her stomach. She had been Catfished.

There was no other explanation. His strange questions about her favourite foods and colours. These were the very things you would get asked in security questions when you forget your password or don't have a card reader for doing things like transferring money to a new account on your banking app. Conscious of this she immediately opened her banking app to check her account for missing money. At first, she couldn't look. She went cold and pins and needles tingled in her hands as she expected the worst. She slowly opened her eyes. As the black digits came into focus, she began to breathe again. No money had been taken but she didn't know what to do and it was almost time for her to start work. Who knows what this person or international criminal ring was able to do with her information! She had described exactly where she lived so they would have her address and how long she had lived there. Her name and age were on her profile. They had her mobile number. They knew where she worked and her position within the company. They had a photo of her they could use for fake I.D. The possibilities were endless and worse case scenarios of losing her home and her job, extortionate debt and even prison for something she didn't do, raced through her mind.

Her heart palpitated, thumping out of her chest. She had to quickly become aware of her breathing to get it under control, as she felt her head get heavy and the pins and needles reach every part of her body, as she hyperventilated. She would have to begin her duties. She had to compose herself. She was pale and distant prompting concerned colleagues to ask if she was ok. There was no way she could tell anyone.

She had been such an idiot. To give all that information without even being fully aware she was doing it. She had heard of woman who had been catfished before on news shows, never suspecting anything like that could ever happen to her. She was always so careful and usually a good judge of character. The realisation that this one stupid mistake could change her life in such a destructive way was too much to bear. She had to stop thinking about it for a while. She couldn't work in this state. She again composed herself trying to function as best as possible considering the circumstances she found herself in. She couldn't even fake a smile. She carried her limp face muscles around, elongating her pasty façade, making her look even more miserable, dragging her feet and looking to the floor. Hiding herself as though even eye contact would expose her as a fool and an object of ridicule. No one could ever know until they had to know. Until the consequences, of the actions of this fool, were exposed and the truth could be concealed   no   longer.

Chapter Six

The Sadness

As Hannah drove into the long communal driveway of her home, she noticed a sign nailed to one of the pillars. It was a 'To Let' sign. She pulled up outside her house and searched on her phone for the Estate Agent's website to find out which of the Coastguard Cottages was being advertised to rent and which of her neighbours was leaving. It was apartment 2B. She noticed George approaching from around the side of the building, so got out of the car and walked towards him. "Have you seen this?" he asked, "What do you think is going on? Do you think Sharon and George are moving on?"

"It's the bottom apartment George," said Hannah delicately.

"No", George murmured after a short pause, "I saw her just the other day. Or was it a week or maybe more. She was getting a taxi" he continued, "a taxi to take her to the shop. She would get them to wait outside the shop and then bring her home again with cigarettes. I would have been happy to get her groceries but not those. Not cigarettes."

"Maybe she has gone to stay with family or into a hospice" Hannah tried to console him. George paused again.

"My neighbours. What's happening to all my neighbours?" George's voice was broken, and his time-worn bloodshot eyes filled like two little pools of water. He raised his hand to his reddened cheek and rubbed his fingers around his chin and jaw, trying not to blink to hold back the tears from rolling down his cheeks in front of Hannah, muffling his speech. "I hadn't spoken to her so much recently. The cold had kept her inside. I always talked to her when she sat out every day. Did you know it was a wig she wore?" George went silent and stood in a daze.

Hannah reflected on how she hadn't noticed any unusual activity. She hadn't seen an ambulance or any cars outside the apartment. They couldn't know if she had died or if someone somewhere was looking after her or even how long she had been gone. They both shared an uncomfortable sense of shame. Grace was alone.

She had no family that called. Her neighbours were her only friends. Hannah didn't know what to say to console George. She excused herself saying she had better go check on Butler. As she turned and walked away, she caught sight of George's dining room curtain drop and swing a little.

It had been a long day. The shock of being duped online had lessened over the day and now seemed much less important. She shuffled in through the front door and Butler dashed around the living room full of energy as he was so happy to see her. He pranced around her feet and wouldn't stop licking her, his tiny hammy tongue tickled her ankles. She almost fell over laughing so she picked him up and kissed his little nose. They went for a well-deserved walk and brought treats for him to enjoy as a reward for being such a tonic.

It was the kind of day that deserved an early night. Bruno was still in Dublin. She received two photos of himself and the others on the conference having a drink. They seemed to be tea total except for Bruno and one of the two pretty females between whom Bruno was sat. She took out her reading glasses to inspect them further.

One of the girls, with long wavy blonde hair and wearing thick black rimmed glasses, was leaning in towards Bruno, with her short skirt and visibly long cleavage. Hannah wasn't jealous or so she told Butler. There were seven of them in total. They appeared to be a pleasant although slightly awkward and geeky looking bunch of techy geniuses. Bruno stood out as ruggedly attractive and the rebellious one with his pint of beer and seemed to be the only one smiling apart from Miss Long Cleavage with her glass of rose wine matching her lipstick. Although she was flattered that he had thought enough about her to send pics, she needed someone to pass the time with and chat with right now.

She sneered as she opened the dating app reflecting on her earlier discoveries about the rogue Scott. She accepted that he must not have been a real person, but she needed someone to be the object of her disgust even if he was fictitious.

Rob, friend of seals, birds and probably all animal-kind seemed like a safe bet. He had sent her some messages about how lovely her long brown hair was and asking if she had any pets. She sent replies and even a photo of Butler that she had on her phone and while waiting for him to send a new reply she sent a message to Dan who was online and replied instantly. Dan looked very attractive and indeed quite young for his age. He had short curly blonde hair, a light tan complexion and nice teeth. He wore tight jeans and an even tighter T-shirt. He had sent her a message four days ago complimenting her photos. His profile description seemed pretty straight forward. He was 6 foot tall. A nice height. Something that stood out was his interest in the supernatural. Perfect for an interesting little conversation. She asked him if he believed in ghosts. He explained that he was open minded but had some experiences which could not be explained and seemed to point towards the existence of ghosts. Hannah decided that he was being diplomatic as he didn't know her and probably had stronger feelings on the matter that would emerge if provoked enough. A strong-minded man would stand by his convictions. Hannah had her own theories for such things and was eager to let Dan know.

She explained that her theory was based on physics and the scientific acceptance that energy could not disappear or be destroyed but only change. Places where there is suspected paranormal activity are usually places where a traumatic event has taken place such as a murder or execution. Energy builds up in the form of adrenaline, electricity or some other form, from the cells and very molecules and atoms and reaches a climax until suddenly a death. Life ceases but the energy still exists. It has nowhere to go and hasn't transformed. It remains there repeating trapped in an endless cycle in a place in space and time waiting to be earthed so it can move on. Being sensed by those sensitive enough to feel it. The electrical energy making the hair on the back of your neck stand up. Hannah romanticized on how it was like a part of the person had been left behind, their passion, their emotions, their energy.

Dan was very impressed. He invited Hannah on his next visit to a haunted house event. On further investigation, Hannah uncovered a possible over fascination in the macabre on Dan's part. He had taken part in seances and Ouija board gatherings. Perhaps Dan wasn't her type after all. On changing the subject, she found out that he was living at home with his parents and was currently unemployed.

Luckily, Dr Rob Dolittle was now online. Hannah closed her eyes and threw her head back, making a wish for him to be normal, employed and most of all a real person.

They had texted each other a few times briefly before but Hannah had to check over their conversation so she wouldn't get him confused with someone else as remembering details was not something she was good at. She was also very bad at remembering names, it was in fact, one of her few foibles.

Rob had a grown-up daughter. He seemed to enjoy boasting about her accomplishments. She didn't live with Rob, so Hannah didn't take too much interest in her but allowed him the time to talk about her.

He explained to her how they chose names for the rescue seal pups at the centre. People had different reasons for choosing them. When it was Rob's turn to choose a name, he would use characters from films he had watched as a child. This opened up whole can of worms for conversation on childhood movies. As Hannah reflected on how scared she had been by some and disgusted at the sexual references in other movies intended for the innocent, she felt quite the prude, but she stood by her convictions. 'If it's a prude I am then it's a prude I shall be!' she proclaimed aloud. She nodded to herself in a self-righteous agreement.

They talked about banshees, rabbits that ripped each other apart, being poisoned by a stepmother, and trying to find One Eyed Willy's treasure while being hunted by a dysfunctional family. They agreed that childhood movies could be greatly disturbing and struggled to think of one wholesome movie between them.

They talked about their dog's and Hannah shared the story of Dorothy, Penny and Harriot, her former pet hens. She had to give them away to a family when her landlord was selling up and she couldn't have chickens at her next place. It was good of the landlord to allow Hannah to keep hens especially as she would let them roam around the walled garden with its four large apple trees and old stone well. However, he was unfortunately a creep. He phoned her up one day while he was eating a meal and drinking lots of red wine. He told her he was moving to Australia to be a scuba diving instructor leaving behind his wife and two children. He asked her to go for a drink adding she had a good figure for swimming and would enjoy scuba diving. During the same phone call, he told her she had four weeks to find somewhere else to live.

Luckily a friend knew someone who wanted a responsible person to look after their property while they moved abroad for a few years. They agreed that Butler would be welcome to move in too, so it all worked out fine in the end.

Rob exclaimed his objection to such a man who would act in such a disgraceful manner. He texted:

It wouldn't have happened
if I had been around

'Ah... extra points for having protective instincts' Hannah thought to herself.

She mentioned that tomorrow was her day off work. Rob was self-employed and worked based on contracts, so he suggested suitably calling in on a client based near Hannah and meeting up for a coffee with Hannah beforehand.

"Perfect!" said Hannah and her next date was   set.

Chapter Seven

The Cheat Sheets

Hannah began her morning by attending her weekly Zumba class. It wasn't a very strenuous class but was more fun and uplifting than a full-on workout. That is why she had chosen it. The Zumba class she used to go to was instructed by a very fit and energetic professional. Everyone who attended seemed just as fit and capable, and they always seemed to know all the moves before they happened, except for Hannah. She would move left instead of right, was always at least two steps behind, refused to jump in the air when instructed to and when she had to spin around her vertigo was agitated, causing her to make a loud retching sound with the sudden nausea. Then, she would spend two days in muscle recovery, sometimes walking like she had a poo in her pants. So, she quit.

Annabella Pasavalova was her present instructor. She was eighty-nine and Columbian. She was small and feisty, had black and white hair and wore a fluorescent pink and green leotard. She had bright eyes, rosy cheeks and a carefree zest for life. Her English was passable. Sometimes she would forget a word mid-sentence and the less fit but friendly class would offer suggestions of what they thought she was trying to say. It was only on a rare occasion that anyone guessed correctly. She had a very unique way of explaining things. She always laughed at herself. She would often say "you know whatta I mean?" but nobody ever did. She would forget moves or think that the music track had finished before it had, but again she just laughed and waved her hands.

Hannah felt confident in this class. She got the moves wrong sometimes but so did almost all the others. Annabella would tell them they were all wonderful and that they had soul and passion, and they were happy to believe it. "As long as you move and feel joy that is all that matter in your life!" she would say at speed in her lovely Columbian accent. She had explained to them one day, that Zumba was the result of "a happy accident". It had been created by choreographer and fitness instructor Alberto "Beto" Perez in Columbia in the mid 1990s. He realised one day on his way to teach an aerobics class that he had forgotten his music, so he used Latino music he had in his car and improvised dance moves. "And so here we are. We have come together because of a happy accident and we make each other happy!" she had said excitedly.

Hannah's favourite moves were during a dance which involved a lot of side stepping and acting out shooting a pistol from the hip. Her least favourite was the one where she had to act out a Spanish love story with moves including her hands like fists in front of her face pretending to weep. It was a tragic love story.

In this morning's class Annabella was excited to introduce a new dance which included twerking. Hannah had never been a fan of twerking and was left feeling like she had pulled a muscle in her buttock. She tried to mask the pain and smile hoping she would be able to walk it off. She didn't want to walk with a funny limp into her date with Rob.

She rushed home from Zumba, had a quick shower and was soon on her way to meet him. She struggled to keep her road-rage under control as she was hangry after her morning exercises. As soon as she got to the coffee shop she wolfed down a slice of lemon drizzle cake and a warm moist chocolate muffin. She had downed her cappuccino to help move the spongy delights down her gullet, so she quickly ordered a second and checked her conversation with Rob in case she had got the time wrong. She sent him a cheeky

I'm inside. You're late! (smiley face)

Suddenly it dawned on her. There were two coffee shops that she knew of, belonging to the same chain on the same road. She, unfortunately, had failed to specify which they were to meet at. She let him know that instant which coffee shop she was at, just in case he was at the other. About two minutes later he turned up at high speed in an expensive car, swerving into a parking space. As he leapt from his car, she could see he was shorter than she had hoped. He was crouched down in one of his pics and in the rest... well they were close ups with only the top half of his body at most. And to be honest she had more of her focus on the birds and animals... how was she to know? He didn't state his height in his profile. She tried to overlook it and move on, but it was a struggle.

He rushed straight in through the wedged open door to where she was sitting, quite out of breath and a little sweaty.

"Hannah?" he said standing over her.

"Hey, I'm so sorry. Did you go to the other café?" She said squirming in her chair.

He smiled but behind his eyes was intolerance and he spoke through his teeth. "Yes, a guy there told me there were three of the same chain along this road", he said indignantly but still smiling. "I see you already have a drink and have eaten." He glanced at the plate with crumbs and the second plate with an empty muffin wrapper. Hannah looked up at him like a naughty child caught with their hand in the cookie jar. "I'll go get myself a drink. Won't be long."

Hannah looked round at the other people in the coffee shop. It was quite busy and looked like she and Rob were not the only people on a first date. She guessed about three of the other couples in there were on a first date.

A girl with long blonde hair was talking to a slim guy with a beard and glasses. He looked like he wanted to say something but was waiting for the girl to take a breath. He was leaned in and looked interested in what she was saying and seemed very attracted to her.

Another girl with long brown hair, light brown skin and a the strap of a small leather purse crossing from shoulder to hip, sat very erect across from a slouching slightly scruffy ginger haired guy. They weren't speaking very much, and both looked suitably awkward and shy. His beard looked very itchy. He kept scratching the skin under it, but perhaps it was just a nervous itch.

The last couple were seated beside a family with three very young active children. They were both quite plump. She had curly black hair, light skin with a naturally healthy complexion. He was black with a shaved head and clean-shaven face. They must have smiled at each other the whole time. The youngest child with two pigtails and a laced, puffed-up pink dress kept throwing her plastic drinks bottle towards their feet from her highchair. They would take it in turns to pick it up and give it back to the amused child.

Rob returned with his drink. A bottle of still orange juice. "Don't you like coffee?" Hannah enquired as he sat down.

"Sometimes, but I'm a little hot today." Hannah observed his clammy red face and said no more about it as she had obviously caused him to rush, due to the lack of information on the location of the cafe. He made himself comfortable on his chair reclining with a man-spread and tapping his knee with his bottle. He looked at Hannah as though he was waiting for her to speak.

"It was a nice morning for a drive," said Hannah. Small talk was not her forte and having been put on the spot she was trying hard to conjure up anything that might warrant a reply.

"Aye" replied Rob putting her creative abilities to the test. She simply couldn't think of anything else to say. There was a moments silence and then Rob stretched back in his chair. "So, what do you think of the hair?" he asked rubbing his head.

"Excuse me?" Hannah responded, as she raised her cup to her lips not sure what to say.

"I don't have much on top which is why I like to design different styles for my facial hair." He used his fingers to twist the ends of his moustache, so they protruded from the sides of his face and curled the ends up just slightly. This is a Handlebar. He smiled in a moment's freeze-frame pose and waited for a compliment.

"That's very nice," Hannah said, curiously watching him amuse himself with his hairy plaything. He rolled the ends in further and wetting his fore finger and thumb he pinched the tiny beard on his chin into a downward pointing triangle.

"This is El Bandito" he said looking very pleased with himself. "My Turkish barber loves me. Everyone else just asks for a clean shave or a beard trim whereas I allow him to practice his art with a blade unrestrained. Do you have a preference on how you like facial hair?"

Hannah had never given it any thought. "It must have taken a long time to get it to such a great length?" It was not the response Rob was hoping for.

"Not really," he said and moved the conversation to a different topic. "I travel a lot and work at times that I choose. I'm very lucky. I don't know how other people work for a company or a boss of any kind." Hannah didn't speak. "I used to have a fear of heights. Until one day I had to inspect a special aerial, on top of a mountain, that I designed. I took a special course to get over the fear where I was lifted by a crane. I was strapped into a harness, and I had to stay there suspended in the air for thirty minutes at a time, until I eventually got used to it and lost the fear. I have to work from heights all the time. I love it now."

"Gosh!" That's very interesting" said Hannah impressed but at the same time feeling a little like her own life and work were pretty mundane in comparison. "It must be amazing overcoming a genuine fear."

There was a silence while Rob contemplated how wonderful he was. Hannah began to fidget as double the amount of caffeine she was used to, from two consecutive cappuccinos, rushed around her veins. "So, you said you had been looking at houses. Do you know what area you want to settle down in?"

"No." said Rob with a confused expression. "I'm not moving. I have a beautiful house by the sea and the dog and I go on a cliff walk almost every day. Why would I move?"

'Oh no!' Hannah thought to herself, 'I've got him mixed up with someone else! What will he think!' Hannah was so embarrassed, she tried not to show it but could feel her lower left eyelid begin to twitch. Meanwhile, Rob didn't look like he was thinking about anything.

"So, you aren't afraid of water then? You must enjoy being in the water if you rescue seals?" she stayed on track only with things she was sure of, and Rob was more than happy to talk about his experience with diving and boats.

Hannah was downhearted. Her eye was twitching at about a hundred revs a second although it didn't seem noticeable to Rob. She couldn't believe this was the same person that she had enjoyed spending so long texting. Now she just wanted the date to be over. She felt an overwhelming urge to move or run or do something with the surplus energy she felt within her body. She had heard enough from Rob about Rob.

She waited for an intermission in the Rob show and took the opportunity to say, "I suppose I should let you get on your way to your meeting," as a subtle hint, but it was futile.

"No, I don't have that meeting for another hour, and I don't need to be on time, they can wait for me," said Rob. Hannah felt like she was being punished for making him go to the wrong cafe. She couldn't bear the thought of having to spend another hour of having to hear more of Rob talking about Rob. Especially as she didn't expect to be seeing him again. At the first opportunity she took the focus off him.

"I was looking around earlier while you were getting a drink and I think I spotted three more first dates taking place in here!"

"Really," Rob replied looking briefly around and then at the floor very disinterested, "Are you being nosy?"

"I just think it can be interesting to watch human behaviours" Hannah retorted justifying her actions. "Don't you find people and relationships fascinating?"

"I prefer animals" he grumbled.

"Well do you see the couple over there? The pretty blonde girl has spoken the whole time and the guy had looked attentive at first but now he is leaning back and looks bored. It's not going well. His body language has completely changed."

Rob looked mildly impressed.

"That couple over there are getting along but are both quite reserved or shy." She gestured towards the second couple. "See how they both have their hands clasped on the table? Sometimes the guy stretches his hands into the middle of the table hoping she will move hers in too then he can try to hold her hand or touch her fingers with his.

He is very interested and wants some physical contact and has been signalling subtly."

Rob said nothing

"Those two are so obviously a perfect couple" she looked towards the last couple and smiled at the pair who were still giggling and saying very little. The couple were getting ready to leave. "Isn't it interesting how certain people just suit certain other people?"

"Do you know where the toilet is?" Rob asked. Hannah pointed to a door.

"It's just in there" she replied. She waited until he had stood up and announced that she would have to go but thanked him and said she had a lovely time. Then she grabbed her coat and made a B-line for the door. Rob stood looking surprised as Hannah marched off and walked straight into the glass door with a large bang to her forehead! An intense dull pain on her skull ensued and a blood rush of embarrassment filled her face.

"Well, that will make up for sending Rob to the wrong cafe!" She maintained her good posture and still facing forward pushed the door open and kept walking as though something mortifying had not just happened.

When she was safely in the car, she phoned her friend Danni and arranged to call on her in time for her lunch break as Danni worked from home. She told Danni about her disappointing date with Rob after having high expectations from their texts. She relived the embarrassment of slamming her head into a glass door and getting him mixed up with someone else who was moving house. After she calmed down from laughing hysterically, Danni had an excellent idea to keep Hannah from repeating her mistake. She should take notes scribbled onto a piece of paper for each person that she speaks to then she can have it with her in short point form while on a date.

"Like cheat sheets!" Hannah exclaimed "what a marvellous idea!" Not that Hannah had ever cheated in an exam. She had just seen others take folded sheets of paper into exams when she was at school!

Danni always had good advice for Hannah. Except for the time she made a blood blister on her thumb to cure her sore throat. She still had a sore throat but had a sore thumb also. And the time she told her to take some scissors and cut a fringe into her long hair. And the other few times there were minor incidences.

Not wanting to waste the second of her two days off, Hannah later chatted with some potential dates, with the aim of procuring herself a coffee date for the following day. She kept some blank sheets beside her and put the name of each one at the top of a fresh page. Despite letting them know she was off tomorrow nobody asked her to go for coffee so she did the asking.

Ralph was the lucky recipient who also had the day off. She arranged to meet him at the same coffee shop where she had met Bruno. Bruno wasn't back from Dublin so there was no chance of bumping into him. She had been keeping in touch with him briefly as he sent her messages like;

Missing me?
and
I will give you a hug when I am back!

He continued to inform her of interesting facts such as 'All crisps expiry dates are on a Saturday'. She checked, it was actually true.

She scanned over her cheat sheets for her date with Ralph: he lived in the city, he was a publisher in his day job, he was a self-employed freelance illustrator outside of his publishing work, he didn't have any children, he liked to travel, he owned his own house, he liked socializing and spending time with family and watching movies. That was everything she needed to know and plenty of material with which to begin a conversation. She folded the piece of paper and put it into the front pocket of her small brown leather satchel.

The next day she was extra early for her date as she had no plans to do anything that morning. She had brought a book to read. She was so engrossed in the story she hadn't noticed it was time for her date until ten minutes after the meeting time. Ralph had given her his mobile number the day before, however, Hannah had decided that exchanging numbers had not worked out well so far, therefore she hadn't put it in her contacts, so she checked the app to see if there was a problem. Ralph had sent a message fifteen minutes earlier asking if they were meeting inside or outside the coffee shop. Hannah felt awful! She apologised and told him she was already inside and had been reading a book and lost track of time.

She observed a man with quite shaggy hair and glasses take a seat by the far window. She tapped on Ralph's profile pic to enlarge it so she could compare the two. The hair of the person in the pic was shorter but she considered that it might have grown since the photo was taken. He looked up and caught her eye. She paused but the guy looked away and after a brief glance around the coffee shop poured the tea from his teapot into his mug, took out his phone and relaxed back into his chair. Hannah left her phone on the table with the app open in front of her so she would notice if there were any replies from Ralph and went back to reading her book.

'I'm here too' came a message eventually. She couldn't see the queue at the counter from her seat so didn't know if he was inside yet or had just arrived and was still in his car. She looked around the coffee shop. The only persons who were alone were the guy at the window who was now busy munching on a muffin and didn't have the appearance of waiting for a date and someone who looked about twenty years older than the pic on the profile. 'I'm around the corner from the counter sitting by the window, reading my book' she texted back. She was beginning to doubt whether he was, in fact, there.

'I'm sitting by the window' he replied leaving Hannah confused. She could not have made it clearer where she was. She was the only person with a book. She suspected the guy with the tea, but why would he act as though he wasn't there to meet someone? She considered that he might be embarrassed but she was not going to be the one to move seats, she been there for the longest time.

Finally, he rose to his feet. He looked over at Hannah and she raised her hand, indicating she was who he was looking for. He carried his mug over to her table. He stood there slouching and looking a little scruffy in an unironed shirt and tatty jeans. "Are you Hannah?" he asked very unsure of himself.

"Yes, I am" said Hannah boosting her enthusiasm for his sake as she felt some pity for his embarrassed state. "Are you Ralph?"

"Yes" he said sheepishly, and he pulled out a chair to sit on, "I was sitting over there".

"Oh, I thought that might be you," she said smiling. He sat with a half-hearted smile looking at her both expectantly and apprehensive as though he was at an interview. So, Hannah began the inquisition. She had been using the cheat sheet as a bookmark. She was holding the book on her lap just under the table, so she opened it and unfolder the piece of paper. "So, you like illustrating. What kind of things do you draw? Is it cartoons or book illustrations?"

"I do any kind of illustrations. I'm freelance working for anyone who needs an illustrator. For fun I do cartoons strips. I like making up characters."

Hannah felt there was a lack of passion for his craft. She asked about his family, and he seemed to enjoy being an uncle to his only niece but didn't go into detail. Next Hannah tried movies. She had hit on his passion. He liked action movies best, but it seemed he would watch almost anything.

A picture formed in Hannah's mind of Ralph on a reclining armchair in a dark room without style. Just some mismatched pieces of furniture. There he was, a stack empty take out boxes, a picture of a naked lady on the wall, with a bowl of microwave popcorn on his lap, scratching his balls with one hand and a remote control in the other. Maybe this was some girls dream but not Hannah's.

She asked if he had travelled anywhere recently but he just seemed to make an annual fortnights holiday, always to the same place in Spain, with family.

"Would you like to ask me anything?" she asked concluding the interview.

"Err...do you have any children?" he said off the top of his head.

"Yes, I have six" replied Hannah mischievously.

"Six?" Ralph puffed up his cheeks, "that's a lot of work."

"It is" Hannah continued quite amused by his reaction. "Three girls and three boys." Ralph took a gulp of his cold tea. "And a chihuahua!" said Hannah, and bringing the date to a close she added, "I really should go walk him in this lovely sunshine, as he has been stuck inside all this time that I have been out."

"OK", said Ralph as he slowly rose to his feet.

"What will you do with the rest of your day?" asked Hannah as she closed the book with the page inside and put it in her satchel.

"I don't know" said Ralph despondently. "I might do some illustrations". They reached the exit of the coffee shop and Ralph held the door open for Hannah to go through.

"Well, that's my car over there. Where is yours parked?"

"The car next to yours" he said so they continued to walk together while Hannah subtly edged away.

"Well thanks. I had a lovely time" said Hannah as she opened her car door, "keep in touch." She sat in the car doing the usual fumbling about in her satchel, only lifting her head to smile and wave as she saw Ralph pull away out of the corner of her eye.

"That's it!" she announced to herself, "dating is a waste of time!" She sat pouting in her car as she thought of how she had squandered her days off, and beautifully sunny one's at that! She drove to the nearby garden centre to pick up some spring flowering plants to add to her garden to cheer herself up.

She was just trying to decide between a white or pink camelia bush when her phone pinged. It was a photo of Bruno at Dublin airport. He was on his way home. A message followed;

I am coming back to you

Hannah laughed. Bruno is always a tonic.

How about you come to watch
a movie with me tonight and
we can fall asleep in each other's arms.

"Typical Bruno," said Hannah rolling her eyes and placing the pink camelia in her trolly. 'It would be lovely to snuggle up to someone' she thought.

Sorry Bruno but I just don't
know you well enough

But you are tempted to come

Then he sent consecutive texts making Hannah's phone ping almost to a tune.

It would be very nice really

Just have you there for a film under a blanket

I would love that

You know you would love to actually

If you would come tonight, tomorrow
I would take you anywhere in the
country you want to go

And you can trust me. You know this.
You can feel it when we meet

     Eventually Bruno was satisfied with meeting up for a walk in the Castle gardens whenever they were both free and during daylight hours. They arranged to meet in two days' time. It gave them something to look forward to and Hannah felt she could give the dating app a break and use her time more wisely. She wanted to be more focused in work too after she had looked so unwell when she last saw everyone.

     She chose the best places to plant in her Camelia and primroses that she had bought, and Butler lay about watching her. She didn't think about dating again until she was getting ready for her   date   with   Bruno.

Chapter Eight
The Loveliness of Ladybirds

It was to be a short date with Bruno. She was on the late shift in work so a stroll in the park with him while he took his break suited them both just fine. The sun was shining warm in a blue sky, but it was cold in the shade. They met up at the Stable-house café and got two takeout teas to drink as they walked. Hannah was not letting go of hers. She had her two hands clasped round it in case Bruno tried to hold her hand. She didn't know if she felt that way yet about him and she didn't want to look like a couple in case she bumped into anyone she knew.

The park was busy with joggers and dog walkers and Hannah wondered if anyone would recognise her from her photo on the dating app as many of the people were guys around her age. Being exposed on an app with many users was leaving her feeling a little uncomfortable and not just today.

"So, you have missed me I think!" said Bruno with a cheeky smile. Hannah smiled. She was glad to be in his company again. Pink blossom was in abundance on the trees that lined the avenue to the pond and drifts of bluebells added splashes of colour in the lush green grass. "Look," exclaimed Bruno as he bent down at the base of a tree and held the point of a green leaf, "The ladybirds are coming out of hibernation. He flicked one onto the palm of his hand and stood up by Hannah so she could see it. Bruno laughed, "Look it is trying to poison me. Do you see the tiny yellow spots it is leaving on my hand? That is its defence against birds. It tastes really, really bad."

"It's beautiful." Said Hannah and she counted the seven black spots on its back.

"Do you know what a herd of ladybirds is called?" asked Bruno with a raised eyebrow ready to impress. Hannah giggled.

"No?" she replied curiously.

"A loveliness!" exclaimed Bruno with pride. "I have found a loveliness of ladybirds just for you."

Hannah observed the picturesque scene in front of her as Bruno knelt down and gently ushered the ladybird back onto the leaf with the others.

They sat on a large rock under the trees. A short gust of wind sent the petals of the blossoms drifting down like soft pink snowflakes. Bruno leaned in towards her as they both looked up at the enchanting pink flurry. Hannah stood up promptly. "What is wrong?" asked Bruno. She couldn't admit she was perturbed by his closeness and preferred a larger gap between them in case he made a move, leaving things awkward between them, but then again maybe she was being too cautious and cynical and should allow herself to relax more.

"I saw a web on the rock!" she said shivering to emphasize her fear with a little drama. I have a phobia of eight-legged things."

"Ahh" said Bruno sniggering.

"It's not funny!" protested Hannah. "Phobias are no laughing matter."

"It's only a tiny web," he said acting unconvincingly serious. "Do you know that spiderwebs don't trigger an autoimmune response and are actually antiseptic and antifungal? Which means you can dress wounds with them, and they contain vitamin K which reduces clotting. Actually! True fact!" Bruno appeared to be more impressed by his knowledge than Hannah. "There is an example of a very large spider," he said playfully, pointing at the ground near her feet. Hannah leapt straight up onto the rock. Bruno stood up and moved to the spot she had been standing on and stomped his foot repeatedly while trying not to laugh at Hannah's reaction. "Oh, I am so sorry", he said sarcastically, "it was only a little tiny tiny twig!" He ruptured into a painful laugh.

Hannah was furious. "We don't use the 'S' word! And I don't think it's very fair...." Before she could finish Bruno threw his arms around her midway, lifting her up and slowly lowering her to the ground, their puffy coats rubbing up a static charge from the friction. Hannah deliberately continued the decent down through his arms until she was crouching and placed her bottom onto the rock.

"Thank you," she said smugly, very proud of how she had handled the situation. "We don't have much time left. Should we circle the pond and walk back by the castle ruins?"

During their walk Bruno pointed out evidence of rabbits and informed her that a group of bunnies is called a 'fluffle'. She was intrigued by his apparent fascination with nature and liked this nurturing side of him.

When they eventually reached the carpark Hannah decided she might have judged Bruno too harshly. Maybe he wasn't just after one thing. There was something nurturing and innocent about him even if he was a little childish and used sexual innuendos.

"Well, I hope you enjoy the rest of your work day Bruno." Hannah kept walking in the direction of her car so as not to allow him time to manhandle her again.

"I will!" Declared Bruno with a loud chipper demeanour. "Now you can come to stay at my house next time we meet." He had a very wide smile with his pearly white teeth on grand display.

Hannah sighed. "I'm done," she said to herself. "You are," she replied. And she drove away.

She reached home just in time to catch Diane fixing her bin into her private outdoor lockup. "How are you today, Francis?" she enquired, poking her head out through her open car window.

"I've been handwashing my clothes for weeks now" she muttered as she locked the padlock with a click. The counsel workers were on strike but now it's been over for three weeks and they still haven't come to collect my broken washing machine! I have written to the local MP!"

"Oh," said Hannah with nothing to add and got out of the car.

"It's my own fault. I have always washed my trainers and slippers together, but the rubber was very worn and they disintegrated and broke the machine. Had to force it open with the claw of a hammer. Water everywhere." She laughed at her own folly. "I can't buy a new one until they take other one away."

Diane reminded Hannah of a lovely lady who called into the pharmacy that she used to work in after she finished university. She had a similar character to Diane. She had diabetes and told Hannah that her favourite toe had dropped off in her slipper and must have been in the slipper for days before she realised. The woman would be in tears laughing about it. Apparently, it had shrivelled up but she would still try to put nail polish on the end of it as though it still had a toenail. They were both very independent women with a good outlook on life and a strange sense of humour.

"Well, I must get ready for work," smiled Hannah as she selected the right door key. "Enjoy the rest of your day Francis!"

Chapter Nine
The Humdrum

Life was pretty much back to normal for Hannah. She returned from the twenty-four-hour coffee bar with her coconut milk cappuccino remnants and sat in the car outside her house, staring at the blue sky with her eyes glazed over. She was still in a daze from the wretchedly sad lyrics of the previously played track on the Sunday Love Songs show, playing on the radio. Now she was listening to the recorded voice messages with song requests for that special person that means so much to someone, or so the jingle claimed.

A man wished his wife of seventeen years happy anniversary and paid her one compliment of being a great mum to their three sons.

Next, a couple wished their daughter luck for her upcoming nuptials. She had just come through a major operation after a long illness and should be recovered by the time she would marry the man who stayed by her side looking after her while she was bedridden.

Lastly, grown up children of an elderly couple congratulated them on their Golden Wedding Anniversary. Fifty years together. The message stated that they had come through many hard times together and had their ups and downs but wouldn't be without each other.

"Really? That's it?" said Hannah quite cross with both the radio and the people who had sent in the requests. "That's the people who are in love? What is love anyway? Staying together for long periods of time or your whole life, for what reason? Being with someone even though they are ill the whole time, taking care of them and being prepared to do that for the rest of your life? Only being recognised for bringing up children well! Surely your life partner is the person who should see and love everything about you as a person, not only your child nurturing abilities. That kind of love certainly isn't for me!" she ended her rant with a snarl.

The DJ played the requested song. "Don't those people know that song is actually about a breakup and trying to mend a broken heart?" Hannah cringed as she listened to the sad lyrics.

'If I find love…' she thought to herself, 'I want to be the most important person in my Love's life. I want them to truly know me. What I like and what I don't.' She turned off the radio.

"What *do* I want?" she asked herself. "Well, let's see…" she replied. She didn't need to give it too much thought. "New romance is exciting and fun, but I want a relationship that that stays that way forever. I want someone who understands me and thinks like I do. Of course, we can disagree sometimes. It is healthy to debate and comprise is important. Romantic gestures, not big one's; not all the time anyway. My favourite chocolate when I am menstruating, some time away when I need a break." She nodded her head in agreement, then lowered the sun visor and slid the mirror cover opened so she could look herself in the eye while she spoke candidly.

"A person in your life should add to your life. You should feel supported and that you can tell them anything. And they should want to make up as soon as you fall out. And cheer you up when you are sad or grumpy. They should always be excited to see you when you have been apart for a short while, even if it is just after you have been in work. And that should never fade. If love is real it wouldn't fade into just being used to each other. That would simply suggest we feel like we are in love in the beginning while there is romance and the excitement of something new, that dies off eventually. Then love isn't even a real thing."

Instead of the clarity of what she wanted Hannah was creating the uncertainty of what was possible. More confused than ever she got out of the car and went inside. Butler leapt from the sofa onto the floor and jumped up around her feet. "Hey little guy!" she said laughing. "We are going for a walk now." She picked him up and he licked her face, wagging his tail and panting. "I'm happy to see you too!" and she giggled at the feeling of his tickling tongue. She took him for a walk round by the marina and they watched a family of seals on the rocks by the coastal path. Hannah grumbled about the requests on the radio and Butler listened. It was a beautiful morning.

That night Hannah decided that if she wanted to find love she could not give up. She must persist and be patient. She knew that lack of patience was one of her foybles but she couldn't remember if she was persistent or not, however, she was willing to give it a go. She got into pjs, put on her 1940's Ragtime album and made herself comfortable. Butler lay beside her with his head on her lap. She opened the app and scrolled down through the many messages that she hadn't checked in some time.

There he was. Henry.

There was something familiar yet different about him.

He was the same height as Hannah with fair hair. He was attractive but not in an obvious way. His profile was different too. He talked about all the things that Hannah had described in her grumble that morning. He wanted to experience something 'more than ordinary'. That's just how Hannah felt!

They chatted briefly and a date was set. He was flexible which was perfect. Trying not to use coffee shops more than twice for different dates in case she got a bad rep, she arranged to meet him in the same café she met Robb and she was specific with her instructions so there could be no mix up this time. This date was an important one. She was so excited she told Danni about it and two of the girls in work. Everyone was excited for her and had their fingers crossed.

The day of the coffee date arrived. Hannah had cheat sheets prepared but she knew she wouldn't need them; she remembered every word they had texted and everything he had put in his profile... she had read them all enough times!

She sat by the window and waited for him. He was prompt. He smiled as he entered the café and made his way straight over to her. "I'm so pleased you agreed to meet me," he said in an undefinable but way cool accent.

Hannah couldn't stop herself from smiling, "I've been looking forward to meeting you so much. Please sit down."

"I think I should get myself a drink first. Would you like anything else?"

Hannah Blushed, "Oh of course! No, I'm fine with my cappuccino thank you." She said feeling like an idiot, but it was too late to retract what she had said. She was nervous. She wanted the date to go well so badly.

Henry relaxed into his seat. "How's Butler today? Have you left him at home while you're out enjoying yourself?"

"He will be fine. I took him for a walk before I left. He needed a nap after that."

"Well, it's a bit strange all this chatting online and then practically a blind date, hoping the other person turns up and is who they presented in their profile." Henry laughed which had a calming effect on Hannah. "So how many dates have you had since you started on that app?"

"Oh, just three," replied Hannah. She would have kicked herself if she was able to when she realised that she had been staring at him the whole time with a creepy smile on her face. She sat back in her chair and tried to look a little more mature and normal. At least she was pleased that she had only met three guys before him and could be honest about it as he had only asked about that specific app.

"Ah, you're my first. I had only signed up and sent you the message and then left it at that until you replied two days later. I don't have much patience when it comes to these things" he smiled.

Henry began to tell Hannah more about himself. He had lived a few years in Canada, a few in Vietnam and before that he had worked in different countries around the world short-term. He had many different jobs. Hannah found it all fascinating and felt quite boring in comparison.

In Canada, he was a counsellor for ex-prisoners. He had worked in other fields of psychology also. They spoke for a long while about psychology, ethics and values changing in the modern world. They had so much in common. Henry cared greatly about the environment and had worked for a conservation agency reintroducing the previously endangered griffon vulture back into the wild, in France. The icing on the cake was when they realised they had grown up in the same area just streets from each other. Henry had returned to help out with his elderly parents and was looking for a house to buy. He was ready to settle down now.

If Hannah had two right hands, she would have hi-fived herself, but she didn't so instead she did it mentally with an internal "You go girl!". She had hit the jackpot! She could never have imagined she could be so lucky.

"It's strange how familiar you look," said Hannah, her voice had a slightly higher pitch now as excitement built up inside her. Then she realised why he looked familiar. He looked very similar to her cousin Johnny. It was uncanny. Then she though he looked a little like her other cousin Michael.

"You have a slight resemblance to my cousin," she said without thinking. "Would you mind if I asked you your surname?"

"I'm sorry?" asked Henry looking puzzled.

"I really just want to check we aren't related," explained Hannah. "I have many cousins. I know all the ones on my mum's side but wasn't close to my dad's side, so I don't know all my cousins on that side of the family."

"I don't know if you are joking or not," said Henry, "but just to put your mind at rest I can tell you that I have only two cousins and I am close to both of them. My name is unusual so I think you would know if we were related quite easily. My family ancestors came from India many years ago, but the name wasn't common there either."

He told her his name and Hannah apologised. She was so relieved and quickly changed the subject, after she laughed with him about how ridiculous she had seemed, but stranger things have happened.

Hannah didn't let it bother her or ruin the date. She was confident that it was going extremely well. It seemed everything they talked about they felt the same way about. Henry was so charming, attractive, funny, caring and showed a genuine interest in Hannah. She couldn't ask for anything more.

She asked him where he was interested in finding a house. He explained that travelling was something he had always done so he didn't need to live too close to his parents and was open to anything. When he found somewhere that he found amazing then he will have found his home.

"You are very lucky to have the ability to choose in that way" she said.

"I am very lucky in many ways" he agreed. Hannah blushed.

But something still didn't feel settled for Hannah. "I'm so sorry," she interrupted as he talked about loving the countryside, "but would you mind telling me the surnames on your mother's side?" You just have such a familiar look."

Henry laughed. He talked her through as much of his family tree as he knew about. "Now," he said, "have I finally put your mind at rest?"

"Yes." Said Hannah, she finally had everything she needed to know, having covered family background checks. Henry was wonderful.

"You're an amazing girl, Hannah" Henry smiled.

Butterflies danced in Hannah's stomach, and she vomited slightly in her mouth, but she still had a smile on her face as she swallowed the bitter acidic taste. Nothing like this had ever happened to her before. All the confusion on love, on whether someone even existed in the world that she could be compatible with. Here he was. Sat in front of her. Perfection personified. Perfect for Hannah atleast. All the disappointment of the dating experiences she had had recently, and in the past, it was just the way things had to be so that time could lead her to this very point in time. Henry was the one. She knew it and she felt that he knew it too.

"Would you like to go for a walk and talk some more Hannah?" Henry asked.

Hannah desperately wanted to but her time with him had been something special. There was so much to take in and she didn't want to forget any of it, and she didn't want to do anything to ruin it. Besides she believed you should always leave people wanting more.

"I'm sorry," she said, "but I really must get back and check on Butler. I've had an absolutely glorious time. I would love to have a walk another time."

"Yes" said Henry as he looked deep into Hannah's eyes and she into his. "I have enjoyed talking with you and finding out about you. It is refreshing to find someone who understands things in the same way I do and has a passion for the same things I do."

He walked her to her car and made no attempt to kiss her or man handle her. Just said goodbye with grace and good manners. They both left thinking about one another and all they had talked about.

The sky looked bluer than usual, and the sun helped release happy hormones in Hannah's body, but who knew, as she was already filled with so much happiness, she could put some in storage, give some to charity, release some into the atmosphere and she would still be fit to burst with happy-atoms. She filled her lungs with cool fresh air, new possibilities, fresh hope, and exhaled. "What a glorious day!"

Chapter Ten

Dancing in the Rain

Hannah got pulled over by the police for speeding. She was doing forty-eight miles per hour in a forty zone on a stretch of the coast road.

She didn't care. Normally she would have felt embarrassed and terribly guilty but today not even that could stop her from smiling. Her happiness was so infectious it was rubbing off on others. She was so apologetic and courteous that she was let off with a warning instead of a speeding ticket.

She continued on her way singing to 80's love ballads at the top of her voice. She didn't know the words, so she made up better ones. She thought about griffon vultures soaring in the sky high above the Alps. She didn't know what they looked like, so she made that up too.

She cringed and blushed when she thought about how she had insisted on knowing Henry's family surnames. Then she burst into laughter as she realised that only she could have the perfect date and then panic that they might be related.

"Henry and Hannah" she said aloud.

"Hannah and Henry" she preferred it that way round.

She sat in the garden with Butler. She didn't know what time it was. She didn't know what day it was. George was pottering about in his garden and kept looking over waiting to say 'Hello' but Hannah was oblivious to anything going on around her. It had been too painfully slow hours since they parted. "I wonder if it's too soon or an unsuitable time to text?" Thus far she had been happy in her daydreams but a plan for when they would next meet was what she wanted now. Something to look forward to. She simply must text him. But what could she say? Something casual...

So when will you be free for that walk?

She deleted it. It was too presumptuous and had no opening line.

Had a lovely time.
Hope you enjoyed it too.

Let's meet up soon

She deleted it. It was unenthusiastic and too generic.

I'm so happy we met up.
I really enjoyed hearing your stories.
You've had such an interesting life.
I'd really enjoy getting to know you more.
If you feel the same, maybe we could
meet up again soon.

Perfect! It was honest. She could wait for his reply and then let him know when she was free. She didn't need to cover everything in the first message.

She waited. She checked the time. She checked if the message had been read…not yet. She waited some more. She checked the time again. Two minutes had passed.

Two minutes turned into two hours. It was the longest two hours of her life! She had texted Danni and sent her his picture that she had screenshot from his profile. She told the two girls in work about how much she liked him and that they would be going on a walk together sometime soon. Talking about him helped to pass the time a little. She tried to think of places they could visit for future dates. New places that weren't tainted by old dates. She planned how she would introduce him to people. She even planned their long-term future together.

When she eventually stopped watching the clock her phone pinged. She expected it to be one of the girls replying but it was *him*. She didn't want to simply open it. She could see the beginning of the message in the notification banner. It was going to be good.

She made herself a salted caramel hot chocolate, put on her classical opera L.P and lit her cherry candles to create the right ambiance. Then, she sat comfortably on the sofa. It was a long message. She shrieked with glee and settled down to read her long awaited reply.

Hey Hannah,
I feel like I have met a kindred spirit in you.
You are so unique and amazing.
I have checked with my parents
and there are no links to your family
names in my family LoL.
I love that you care so much about the world,

And it is so good to meet someone that
is so open and honest and unintentionally funny.

Hannah paused and tried to think what she had said or done that was funny. She could think of nothing, so she read on as his apparent declaration of love at first sight made her heart swell into warm pink squashy marshmallows!

You are one of the most independent
and spirited girls I have ever met.
If I was looking for a friend, then
everything would be perfect but I'm
afraid I'm not as I have friends in
abundance. I'm sure someone with
everything you have to offer will have
no problem finding someone worthy
of you. Best of luck.
Henry.

Hannah couldn't move. If she had seen a ghost in a frog-suit blowing raspberries she would have been less shocked!

She didn't understand. What was wrong with him? Didn't he know that you don't meet people you connect with like this every day?

Some people never meet anyone who understands them as much as they understood each other. Didn't he understand that they were meant to be together?

She knew it must be a mistake, a horrible mistake. She read the last line again. "What was he looking for?" she cried. She so was angry. He was wrong. "Friendship is how the best relationships begin! He is stupid and arrogant!" Then she felt bad for saying cruel things about him.

Her anger turned to sadness. She burst into tears. Butler looked up at her but made no attempt to comfort her as he could sense that she wouldn't be receptive. She felt lonely. But she was just as she had always been. She wanted to reply and tell him he was wrong. She had never met anyone like him before. Someone that she was so certain she could love and spend the rest of her life with.

She felt lonelier than she had felt her whole life. She was missing something that she didn't even know that she wanted. It felt like she was in one of the old black and white movies that she had cried watching many times. Life was cruel.

She was embarrassed by how she had behaved about him. How she had told her friends she had met someone she really liked, and they felt the same about each other, and how perfectly perfect her new guy was!

The sky outside had grown dark, and rain began to fall. It hit the windowpane and ran down like the world was crying too.

She needed some air. She stood up and walked to the backdoor grabbing three tissues from the box as she passed. She put on her puffy coat and pulled the hood up over her head. As she stepped out into the garden, she could see raindrops were making large wet circles on the crazy paving. She sat on the seat under the trees in the dank grey area. She looked back at her house with the peeling paint on the large sash windows and the cracks on the tall chimney pots, seeing only flaws that she had never noticed before.

The rain got heavier until it felt and sounded as though someone was throwing clusters of tiny stones over her. Leaves on the trees held water until they conceded and let go of their load dropping small blasts of cold water under the weighted pressure.

Everything felt so unfair. She wanted to be someone to somebody. Why couldn't she have that? Why did nobody feel that way about her?

A little robin landed holding onto the side of the bird bath in which water splashed upwards as the raindrops pelted it. The little bird shook itself and its scraggy feathers plumped up, so it was three times its original size. It looked at Hannah as though it was a tiny friend trying to make her laugh, but she didn't even smile.

She felt a sadness in her heart and in the pit of her stomach. Tears and rainwater dripped off the end of her nose as she sat still.

Then she listened. There was a strange scratching sort of noise. Perhaps an animal trying to find shelter. She listened some more. It wasn't that kind of noise. Someone else was there. It was a foot sliding along the wet ground. She could hear a faint sort of humming. She made her way quietly to the shrubs at the side of the garden and peered between the trunks of the fruiting cherry trees.

Diane was dancing in the rain. She was dressed in a black flowing dress that had a low cut back in the stiff tight bodice, which had forced her breasts upwards softly bouncing under her chin as

127

she moved. Her cheeks were a rosy pink, and her lips were deep red and glossy, making them appear large and plump. Her black fringe was held back with a white rose fascinator revealing large black curled faux eyelashes. Her pearl embellished dress swayed as she twirled with her invisible dance partner. She giggled and blushed as he paid her a compliment. She was glowing with happiness as the wet dress began to cling to her legs. Hannah could see she was wearing black high heels with something that made them sparkle. She wished she could join her, she looked like she was having so much fun, but she stayed hidden until she felt like a stalker and crept away wiping her nose with her soggy bundle of tissues. Inside, she dried herself with a towel. Her moment of sadness had passed, and she was no longer caught up in an overly dramatic dismally romantic storyline that was mainly from her imagination and was simply rejection. She was herself again. She was Hannah.

Chapter Eleven

The Epiphany

An Epiphany is a moment of sudden and great revelation.

For Hannah it was the realisation that she was happy. In fact, she was happier than most of the people she knew. Furthermore, she always had been.

Hannah woke up on a Wednesday morning much like any other. She stretched every muscle in her body that she believed it possible to stretch voluntarily. Some crunching and popping sensations reassured her that everything was in order.

She opened her bedroom curtains and congratulated the blue sky on its splendour, then slid the sash window upwards and inhaled the fresh crisp air.

After slipping her feet inside her fluffy slippers she went for her morning pee and took Butler outside into the garden so he could have his morning liquid squirts on the plant pots and tree bases.

She had just brushed petals from the garden chair and sat down to drink her coffee when her phone pinged. It was Bruno.

Good morning Beautiful ... Missing me?

She looked at Butler. "I agree" she said and text back

Nope

You are an imp!

She looked at Butler again. It was obvious that Butler was thinking the same as her.

Impertinent, impossible, impolite
and also an imp! Actually!

She sent a reply to that...

Do you remember you told me you
donated blood Bruno? Do you
know it could be in someone else's

Then she blocked him and deleted the chat. She smiled and slurped her coffee so loud she alerted George to her position.

"Morning!" he shouted from his hostas. "The snails have been loving the weather and all the new leaves trying to break through!"

"Yes" she replied with a short wave avoiding another conversation about the state of the drainage since they raised the road in 1968.

A tiny bluetit landed on the side of the birdbath then took a dip in the rainwater splaying its tail feathers and wings then shook vigorously and flew back into the trees. Hannah had read that humans often wrongly attribute human emotions to birds and animals, but she didn't care about that flawed view. She knew the little bird was happy. "Why would someone keep a bird in a cage? All they want to do is fly!" she said. "Freedom is happiness" she replied.

She was on the evening shift so wanted to make the most of the sunny day. She quickly got ready and left with Butler to go for a long drive. She grabbed hold of the large knocker and pulled it shutting the door behind her.

She turned round just in time to catch sight of Francis as she floated along in the distance in a lilac dress. She had her small backpack on which meant she was off to catch the train probably to the beach or one of the houses of the grand estates that she loves to visit. She was too far to make out her face, but Hannah knew she was smiling, because she could see the sun had caused her raised cheeks to show in the long shadow she cast, when she turned her head.

"Butler!" she said, "We are going for a drive." She opened the car door and waved to George who was now tying his drooping clematis more securely to its trellis. She caught sight of George's wife looking at him from the window, but she couldn't wave as she moved away quickly when she saw Hannah looking.

Hannah jumped into her dinky little car and plugged her phone in to play her 'Bordeaux and Beyond' playlist on shuffle. She pressed the button that slowly retracted the purple fabric roof allowing the sun to drench the car in rich warm light. She didn't know if she would meet someone or if she wanted to at least until the time was right. Anyway, she wasn't sure that any man deserved her. Apart from some very minor flaws she was practically perfect! For now, she just wanted to be Hannah. Loving life, learning new things, enjoying her work and spending times with friends. Oh, and Butler. She didn't mind picking up his poo or him licking her face or carrying him over the deep puddles. How many girls can say that about their guys? And he was always so happy to see her and was very protective of her. He was her true love. Her life was whole. She had put on pause so much in pursuit of something she didn't really want. "Well not anymore" she said winking at Butler and no word of a lie; he winked back.

The End

Printed in Great Britain
by Amazon

14772453R00082